A Christmas on Nantucket

and other stories

Carol L. Wright

Cozy Den Press

Publisher

A Christmas on Nantucket

and other stories

Cozy Den Press

Cover photo: Nantucket Christmas, reproduced under license from DepositPhotos.com

Author photo © 2019 by Emily Murphy Photography. http://EmilyMurphyPhotos.com

ISBN: 978-0-9742891-5-1

Library of Congress Control Number: 2019952208

Printed in the United States of America.

A Christmas on Nantucket

and other stories

for GG and Teddy

Table of Contents

A Christmas on Nantucket

The mood in the church was somber for the twenty-third of December. Mourners filed out, heads down, and drew their coats closer as they made their way to their cars. Inside, the new widow cradled the urn containing her husband's ashes and fought back her tears.

"Come home with us, Laura," the widow's mother offered. "Brian wouldn't want you to spend Christmas alone."

Laura grimaced. She realized that from now on, people were apt to tell her what Brian would or would not want, and she could no longer check with him to see if they were right. She shook her head.

"No thanks, Mom," she said. "Besides, I won't really be alone, you know."

The older woman looked at the urn and frowned. "Well, let us know if you change your mind."

Laura struggled to find a smile, but could not. She drew in her breath. "Thanks, Mom, but I'll be okay."

"I'll call you then," her mother said.

"No, please don't," Laura said with more vehemence than she intended. When she saw her mother's expression, she softened, saying, "I'll call you, okay?"

The mother squeezed her daughter's arm and nodded before taking her husband's elbow and leaving the church.

Laura took the urn to the home she and Brian had shared for a decade and a half. She placed it on the mantle and poured a glass of wine.

"To us, darling," she said, raising the glass and placing it on the mantelpiece.

Laura had known this day would come, and thought she was better prepared. She shook her head, blinking back her tears. After lighting a fire in the fireplace, she collapsed in a chair, losing herself in the scent of smoke, the spikes of flame, and the popping of the wood. Her mind drifted to the past few months.

It had been a wonderful summer. Brian quit smoking, yet lost weight without even trying. He looked more like the twenty-five-year old Laura had married than a man of forty.

They stole away for a week's vacation on Nantucket where they had honeymooned. They spent their days on the beach, dined on lobster, and made love like newlyweds. It was as if the fifteen years of marriage, building careers, enduring miscarriages, and surrendering to child-lessness all melted away. At midlife, they felt the joys of youth and health and vigor.

When they left the island, they did what they had done fifteen years before: they each threw a penny into the water as they passed the lighthouse at Brant Point.

"Now we're sure to come back," Brian said, citing the old legend he had read about as a boy. "If you toss a coin into the water as you pass Brant Point, you are certain to return."

Then, shortly after Labor Day, Brian complained of a dull ache in his upper abdomen that radiated to his back. The doctors ran several tests before giving them the diagnosis: pancreatic cancer. Only five percent of victims survive five years, they said, and Brian would not be among them. His cancer was advanced. He had only three to six months.

At first, Brian continued to work, but the pain worsened. Once a week, he went in for chemotherapy. It could not cure his cancer, but it helped relieve his pain.

In October, he went on disability, and Laura took a leave of absence. They tried to make the most of the days and hours they had left. On good days, they would go for a drive to admire the fall colors, buy apples at a nearby orchard, or pick their own pumpkins at a local farm. On bad days, Laura held his head as he vomited, read to him, and watched him sleep.

By mid-November, Brian looked as sick as he was. He was jaundiced and thin. They celebrated their last Thanksgiving at home, grateful they could spend it together. By the first week of December, they knew that Brian would not make it to six months. They needed to finalize their plans.

"I'd like my ashes spread on Nantucket," Brian said, then added with a grin, "I wouldn't want to waste that perfectly good penny I threw overboard."

Then, on the first day of winter, the darkest day of the year, Brian died. It was Laura's turn to feel the pain in her abdomen, as if someone had reached in and pulled out something vital.

Laura went through the motions of carrying out Brian's final arrangements. The cremation, the funeral, all went according to plan.

"But now what?" Laura asked the urn. "You weren't supposed to die so soon. How am I supposed to celebrate Christmas without you?" She thought she had used up all her tears, but there were more.

Sleep that night did not come easily. Rising early, Laura went to her computer and made a few arrangements. She threw a suitcase in the car, put the urn in a shoulder bag, and buckled it into the passenger seat. Then she headed east.

Christmas Eve traffic clogged the interstates and choked the tollbooths. The brooding sky gave way to occasional fits of rain, then sleet, slowing her progress. Laura pushed on with only the *thwap-thwap* of windshield wipers for company. After nightfall, she reached Hyannis. Parking at the Steamship Authority, she bought a ticket for the ferry. Two hours later, she could see Brant Point Light.

Disembarking at Nantucket, Laura grabbed her bags and walked up the dark, empty street. A cold wind whipped through her coat and stirred the dusting of snow that had settled among the cobblestones. All the shops were closed, some for the season, but a few scattered homes were aglow with Christmas lights. She trudged on to the door of the guest house where she and Brian had stayed twice before. The sound of voices singing Christmas carols wafted from within. She braced herself and opened the door.

The singing stopped, and five pairs of smiling eyes turned toward her. "Merry Christmas!" someone shouted. Laura nodded.

"Welcome back," the proprietor said, reaching for registration forms. "I was beginning to wonder if you were going to make it. Where's your husband?" He looked up and caught his breath. "Oh, uh . . . sorry," he said when he saw what Laura carried.

A strained silence hung over the gathering until Laura found her room. As she closed the door, she heard the music begin again, but it was more subdued. She readied herself for bed, laid the urn on the pillow next to her, and fell asleep.

Laura woke at dawn, and pushed the curtains away from windows etched with frost. White clouds skidded across a deep-blue, New England sky, and the sun glinted off a thin coating of snow. A white Christmas.

Laura joined her fellow lodgers at breakfast. She bypassed the coffee pot and took her orange juice and muffin to the sun porch. From there she could see the old whaling town decked out like a miniature Christmas village. Why had she and Brian never come in the winter before?

After breakfast, Laura returned to her room. She put the bag with the urn over her shoulder and went out.

She strolled to the beach, now a blend of snow and sand. Standing on the deserted shore, she spoke to the waves.

"Here we are again, Brian," she began. "You said we would come back here someday." She wiped tears from her eyes, and blamed them on the wind. "You said you wanted your ashes spread on Nantucket, but you didn't say where. I think this is the place." She paused, as if waiting for a response.

She looked at the urn and nodded, then walked to the water's edge. She opened the container and sprinkled Brian's ashes into the receding waves. "I love you, Brian," she whispered as she watched the ashes mix with sea and sand and tears, and fade from view.

She stood a moment, looking out to sea. Then, she felt a fluttering, like a butterfly in her abdomen. She placed her hand below her belt and waited to see if it would happen again.

Her grandmother would call it "quickening"—the first small sensation of the life growing within her.

Four and a half months. She had never had a pregnancy last this long. This proof of life was a gift, she thought. It was Brian's last Christmas gift to her. For the first time in days, she smiled. Their string of tragedy had ended. This child, Brian's child, would live.

Laura had wanted to tell everyone about the pregnancy, but Brian said no—not until they were sure that, this time, it was not a prelude to sadness. Finally, she was sure.

Laura caught the noon ferry back to the mainland. As the boat left the dock, she pulled out her cell phone and called her mother.

"Merry Christmas, Mom," she began. "Yes, I'm fine. . . . No, Mom," she said, her hand on her belly. "I'm not alone. . . . Mom, I have some good news to tell you and Dad."

She smiled and reached into her pocket. And, as they passed Brant Point Light, she tossed two pennies overboard.

American Flyers

You'd think a grown man would know better. But there's something about the first big snowfall of the year that makes a kid out of all of us—well at least of me. We got eight inches overnight. And now I have a kid of my own to share it with.

George is inexhaustible. At four, he's fully aware of the purpose of a snowball. Even if he needs a little help forming one, once I pack it for him, he flings it at my legs before I have a chance to back away.

We build a huge snowman in our front yard—at least on George's scale it's huge. He stands just off the sidewalk so he can keep an eye on the neighborhood. I take off my scarf to wrap around its neck as George goes inside to beg buttons and a carrot from Mommy. No top hats in our closet for the final touch, but he makes a very respectable snowman—or snow *person,* as Mommy apparently told George it's supposed to be called.

When we go inside, though, all the PC crap is forgotten. The woman made us grilled cheese sandwiches and tomato soup. Just like the TV commercials.

We peel off our wet coats and, after the mandatory five minutes at the bathroom sink to wash our hands "thoroughly, this time," we're back for inspection, and the joy of comfort food.

I look out the window and see it's starting to rain. Just a bit. Not enough to melt our snow person. No need to concern George about that.

When lunch is over, George struggles to put his coat on again. How come he never tries to do it by himself when we're running late for church?

Mommy puts the brakes on George's ambition. Not so soon after lunch, she says. It's quiet time. But I had promised George we'd go sledding. Can't break a promise, right?

Mommy says it's raining anyway. We can go after George's nap if the rain has stopped. Fine by me. A little quiet time doesn't sound so bad— especially if George is asleep, and Mommy isn't.

Georgie's "nap" consists of lying on the bed while Mommy reads to him. Oh well. I get some sleep, at least.

The rain has stopped, so George and I get into our coats. I pull out the new toboggan and remove the big red bow from Santa.

"Okay, kiddo. Let's go sliding."

George has never gone on a toboggan before. And I know the perfect hill. George, the toboggan, and I pile into my car and I drive to the golf course. This is going to be great.

It's turned colder again, and the roads are a little slick with frozen rain. Fortunately the ruts left by uncleared snow give me all the traction I need. We pull up on the road by the golf course at the top of what I know will be an epic hill.

"This is it, Georgie."

We get out and put the toboggan on the snow. It starts to slide away from me right away. It's as eager as we are.

Keeping a foot on the back end of the sled, I place George in the front, then get in behind him. As I prepare to instruct my son in the finer points of steering, I put my feet up on the wood. And we take off.

There's a crust of ice on the unbroken snow, and the hill is even steeper than I thought. We're not just sliding, we're plummeting down the hill. George screams. I *think* it's with delight.

We gain speed as we go: down the hill, across where the rough might be, onto the buried fairway. I've gained enough of my senses to throw my weight in time to avoid the sand trap, only to realize that we're now rocketing towards the woods. There's no traction—no friction. We're sailing right for a tree. *Good God. I have to save my son!*

I pull my feet off the rails and jam my heels against the snow. The ice is hard and barely dents as we whiz past, but my knee complains. Once more, with all my effort. I ram my foot into the ice, burying a heel in the snow and spinning the toboggan to a stop, just in time to hear my leg bone snap.

I can now see George's face as I scream every word I know I'm not supposed to use in front of him. It hurts too much to move—and too much to stay still. George's happy face turns to alarm. Then he bursts into tears. *No kidding, George.* Tears are the only appropriate response if you don't know swear words.

Fortunately, we aren't the only ones on the course that day. An elderly couple is cross-country skiing with their Labrador Retriever. As they approach, all I can say is, "Gotta cell phone?"

So now I'm home after three days in the hospital and surgery to set my leg. It will be several weeks before I can walk without crutches. And several more before I'm able to even think about going sledding again.

With any luck, it will be an early Spring.

Grandma's Vegetable Soup

The year I was in eighth grade, my piano teacher, Mrs. Cook, suggested I take pipe organ lessons. She assured me that learning the pipe organ was a guarantee of employment for life, and since hymns were already a part of my piano repertoire, it seemed like an easy transition.

Mrs. Cook had arranged for her students to use the organ at the Congregational church in the center of town to practice, and Grandma lived only a couple of blocks away.

"This could work out great," Mom said. "You can go to Grandma's after school, then spend an hour at the church, then go back to her house for dinner."

I wanted to take organ lessons, and I loved Grandma, but when Mom suggested that I spend so many hours at her house, I was—I hate to admit it—afraid I would be bored. *Well,*

I thought, *I could at least get a head start on my homework.*

So with a shiny, new key to the church entrusted to me, I was ready to begin.

Every Tuesday and Thursday after school, I walked the mile and a half into town to spend an hour with Grandma before my late-afternoon practice time.

The walk was great fun during that New England autumn. I loved the deep blue skies and rustling through piles of leaves on warm, Indian-summer days. Grandma and I found several ways to pass the time. She taught me to play cribbage, and, surprisingly, it turned out that we had a lot to talk about. Then, she would prepare a small dinner while I was at the church. I almost never got any homework done before Dad came to pick me up.

But that winter was especially cold. And girls had to wear skirts to school. Despite my hem-length woolen coat and my calf-high boots, I lost all feeling in my toes well before I reached Grandma's house. Was playing the pipe organ really worth all this?

One cold, winter day, I trudged over snowy paths, crunched along icy sidewalks, and scaled crusted snow banks between school and Grandma's. By the time I reached her door, my legs were numb. But I felt warmed by the smell of onions cooking in butter—the beginning of Grandma's vegetable soup.

I ached for the comfort of the indoors, but my frozen hands inside stiff gloves couldn't turn the knob. So I knocked.

"You don't have to knock," she said greeting me with a squeeze, her faced creased in a broad smile. "Come in and warm up."

She took my coat and hung it up while I rubbed my legs to restore the feeling. As they thawed, I could finally sense how cold they had become.

"Come help me chop," Grandma said, steering me toward the kitchen. She had already cut the carrots and potatoes. My job was the celery. "Make sure you keep the pieces as close to the same size as you can so they'll cook evenly," she admonished.

I took an apron from the hook, washed my hands, and set to work. The chopping took a while; it's hard getting those pieces uniform in size. Grandma checked my work and pointed to a few too-large pieces I had overlooked.

When I got her "okay" wink and nod, I dumped the celery into the pot. Grandma stirred it in with the onions and added carrots. Once they had a chance to soften, she added the other ingredients: beef broth, tomatoes, salt, pepper, parsley, soy sauce, Worcestershire sauce, paprika. There was no beef in her vegetable soup; that was a luxury Grandma couldn't afford.

"Okay, now," she said, her tight, blue-white curls loosening in the humid kitchen. "Stir everything together—*slowly*—so that it's evenly mixed." I tried to stir slowly but still slopped some broth out of the pot. It sizzled and smoked on the stove. She arched a brow and handed me the sponge.

Under her watchful eye, I continued stirring until all was blended to her satisfaction. Wiping her hands on her apron, she said, "Wonderful. I'll put the kettle on, and we'll have some tea while the soup comes to a boil." Tea with Grandma made me feel grown up, even though I added sugar—something she would *never* do.

By the time we finished our tea, the soup was boiling, and it was time to go to organ practice. But I rebelled at the thought of going back out into the wintry day.

"Do I have to go?" I used my best argument. "It's so cold in the church that it makes it hard to play." Then, when I thought she might relent, I hit her with what I was certain would be a winner. "I *could* just stay here, and we could play cribbage."

Grandma hesitated but shook her head. "Your parents are paying for your lessons. The least you can do is practice."

Darn it. Guilt. It worked every time.

"But," she continued, "I'll come with you if that will help."

I smiled.

Grandma turned the heat down so the soup could simmer while we were gone. After wrapping ourselves up in coats, scarves, hats, and gloves, we walked in a gathering dusk past the post office, pharmacy, dry cleaner, hair dresser, bakery, and package/grocery store to the old, white-steepled church.

I unlocked the door, and together we went into the unheated sanctuary. We were out of the breezes, but in the still air it felt even colder than it had outside—like stepping into a freezer.

We could see our breath as I turned on the lights. I kept my coat on to play, but had to remove my scarf and gloves, and set my boots aside to put on my special organ shoes with a smooth sole and broad two-inch heels. Grandma sat in a pew to listen as I fumbled my way through hymns and anthems. She endured my clumsy feet sliding along the foot pedals, the pauses to open or close stops a chord or two too late, and the dissonance caused by cold pipes slipping out of tune. Each error reverberated off the sanctuary walls. I could almost see the stained-glass saints cringe.

After I had tortured the organ long enough, I packed up my hymnal and sheet music, took off my organ shoes and slipped into my now cold boots.

"I always love hearing you play," Grandma said as we started the walk home in the winter darkness. "You sound pretty good."

Bless her heart. I knew better. My fingers were too numb to be nimble, and my too-big feet never seemed to hit the right pedal, but I thanked her anyway.

On our way home, we stopped in at the bakery. The smell of breads, cakes, and pastries reminded me of how long it had been since lunch.

We picked up a baguette—warm from the oven. Even though I knew it wouldn't be warm by the time we got to Grandma's, it would still have its delicious crust and soft center. Perfect with vegetable soup.

We could smell the soup before we opened the front door. I dashed into the kitchen to stir it, mixing the tomatoey bubbles on top with the vegetables beneath. Steam clouded my glasses and warmed my frozen cheeks.

"It's done, isn't it?" I asked Grandma when she caught up with me.

She stirred it and made a face like it needed to simmer a bit more.

"Oh no. How much longer?" I tried not to whine.

"Just long enough for you to set the table," she said, tousling my hair.

I put our placemats on the old drop-leaf table, set out soup spoons and butter knives, and placed bowls onto dinner plates. Grandma poured us drinks and laid out the bread and butter.

After she ladled the soup into bowls, and we said grace, I took a spoonful and blew on it, willing it to cool enough not to burn my tongue. I never waited long enough. But even with a scalded mouth, I could savor the blended flavors, enjoy the textures of tomatoes, carrots, potatoes—and uniformly cut celery. No meal could be better.

That spring I told Mrs. Cook that the pipe organ and I were parting ways. I'd find some other means of gainful employment when I grew up.

Grandma didn't mind. "I guess from now on I'll just have to come over to your house to hear you play the piano," she said. That suited me fine.

But once the new school year started, I still stopped by Grandma's a couple of days a week after school. And on cold winter afternoons we'd play cribbage and chat while her vegetable soup simmered on the stove.

A Mother's Gift

It was time to call the family, they said. My mom, Jane, would not survive this hospitalization.

The news was not unexpected, but terrible all the same. We'd been losing Mom by inches for months—years, really.

First, she had trouble remembering things—even long-cherished family stories. Next, she had trouble remembering people. She asked if I ever heard from her brother who died a decade before. She didn't recognize my brother. She told my sister she hadn't seen me in weeks, when I had just visited her earlier in the day. Each stage was painful, yet each was better than the one to follow.

In recent months, she had stopped speaking. The only real contact she had with others was through hugs. She melted into our arms, soaking up the love. At least we still had a way to reach each other.

Dementia attacked not only her brain but her body. She became frail, and her ability to swallow was compromised. After inhaling food into her lungs, she contracted aspiration pneumonia. Even with the help of modern science, she was not equal to the fight.

I sat with her in the sterile hospital room with my husband. Our children, who now lived far from home, had gathered close, while my siblings traveled from even greater distances. The rhythmic whoosh of the ventilator reminded us that without its support, Mom would no longer be with us by the time they all arrived. I knew she would have wanted mechanical assistance to help her wait for them, even though she couldn't express consent.

Family was most important to her. She loved children—especially babies. I'd known that all my life. She told me that she had once thought she always wanted to have a baby in the house—but, of course, babies grow.

She was just as in love with her grandchildren, having a special relationship with each. My daughter was her first; my son her second. Their cousins followed, increasing her joy in immeasurable ways. But it had been many years since our family had any babies.

Not long after my daughter Jessica married, Mom said to her, "I don't know if you're planning on children, but if you are, could you not wait too long? I want to meet my great-grandchildren."

My daughter assured her they planned to have kids within a couple of years.

"Well, you never know," Mom said. And she had a sixth sense about such things.

* * *

We never told Mom that Jessica and her husband, Mark, were having trouble conceiving. They started trying when Mom still lived independently. Years passed, and while Mom moved into assisted living, and then to a "memory care" facility, they still had no success. They consulted a fertility clinic that identified the problem and told them they would need to use *in vitro* fertilization—IVF. There was no other way.

But IVF is expensive and carries no guarantees. Over the past year, they had tried three times. Painful hormone shots forced my daughter's body to produce, in one month, a quantity of eggs that would usually mature over three years. All the while, expenses rose. On the first try, they did not get a single viable embryo. On the second and third, they had embryos that grew, but did not develop into blastocysts—the optimum stage of development for transfer. They transferred some anyway, but none implanted. No pregnancies.

Each failure was, for them, a little death—a death of hope that they would be able to have children. With their insurance coverage exhausted, and their bank account drained, they were losing hope of ever creating life together. They sought counseling to help deal with their grief, and their therapist had them write letters to the child they would never have.

And now my daughter's grief was compounded by knowing that she was losing the grandmother she adored without ever giving her the great-grandchildren we had all hoped for.

* * *

People started arriving. My husband and son went out to meet my sister and nephew in the hall. Jessica and I were alone with Mom.

We had always been a terrific threesome: best friends as well as family. A strong, maternal line of strong, determined women: mother, daughter, and granddaughter. It was a connection we all cherished. And we knew this was the last moment we would ever be alone together.

Although Mom had been nearly unresponsive since arriving at the hospital, I hoped she was still aware enough to hear me as I spoke.

"Mom, I want to tell you something. Jessica and Mark have been trying to have children for a long time, but they have run into an infertility problem. They've gotten help, but it hasn't worked."

Mom's eyes were open. Was she listening? Was she understanding?

"So," I continued, "when you get to the other side . . . if there's anything you can do to help, it would mean so much."

For the first time since arriving at the hospital, Mom raised her head off the pillow and looked at me. Words were out of reach, but her expression spoke to us in a combination of surprise and pain. She hadn't known about any of this. How could she, when she could barely recognize us? Yet, it was clear to me that, somehow, she had understood.

She laid her head down again as family from the hall bustled in. Each had their moments with Mom, holding her hand and kissing her cheek. After everyone had a chance to say goodbye, the hospital removed the ventilator. Soon after, Mom was gone.

* * *

A month later, Jessica tried IVF for the fourth time. Mom had left her enough money to make it possible. Compounding her anxiety was the knowledge that this was very likely the last chance they would ever have. Even the fertility clinic didn't support a fifth attempt.

They went through the steps: many days of painful injections, a closely timed trigger shot, egg retrieval, fertilization, pain management. Too weary from disappointment to allow themselves the treachery of hope, they waited for the report from the clinic.

The hardest part for me was waiting for them to call. I wanted to know everything, but I didn't want to intrude on what I knew was a difficult time. When Jessica finally called, I was thrilled to hear that they had a few nascent embryos. But they had produced embryos that looked promising on the first day before. The clinic scheduled a transfer for four days later, but could not promise the embryos would last that long. All anyone could do was hope they would thrive.

As the days passed, the news stayed hopeful. Each embryo was still growing on day two, but fast growers did not necessarily mean they were healthy. Sometimes a fast starter would peter out just as quickly.

By day three, there were fewer embryos, but some were coming along in textbook fashion. We wouldn't know anything more until transfer day. The clinic did not disturb the embryos on day four, hoping they might develop better if allowed to rest.

When day five dawned, I startled awake, remembering the last wisps of a dream. In it, Mom was holding a baby who cooed and smiled into her teary eyes. She kissed the baby in her "favorite kissing spot," on the inside of its wrist. Then she looked at me and smiled.

The transfer was scheduled for early that morning. I didn't allow more than a couple of feet between me and my phone, hoping that when it rang, there would be good news. When it finally arrived, the news was better than I could have hoped. Not only did they still have viable embryos, for the first time, they had two healthy blastocysts. They transferred both to double the chance of implantation. But we wouldn't know the results for two weeks.

It was a long fortnight, not knowing whether to encourage Jessie to hope, or help her brace for disappointment. We talked about adoption. We talked about living without children. We shared laughs and tears and the terrible helplessness of waiting.

We stayed with them for part of the second week to be there to celebrate or console them when the day came for the blood test to measure hormone levels. Another early clinic appointment to draw blood. Another seemingly endless wait for results. We baked and settled in with warm cookies and glasses of milk, watching a sappy movie while waiting for the phone to ring.

When the nurse called, she didn't waste time on pleasantries. "You have high levels of pregnancy hormones," she said. "It looks like you're having a baby!"

She'd been so braced for disappointment that Jessica hardly knew how to react. Days later, her first ultrasound confirmed it. One of those precious embryos had implanted.

The doctor was bewildered. "What did we do differently?" she asked.

We knew it wasn't the science that was different. They had a bit of help from heaven.

* * *

Less than a year after Mom left us, her great-granddaughter was born—another strong woman in the line. They named the little girl Angela Jane for the angel named Jane who helped her come to be.

The first time I held our miracle child, I kissed her wrist in Mom's sweet spot. That was the first moment I noticed the pale-pink, heart-shaped mark.

"Oh look," the nurse said. "An angel kiss." She couldn't have known how right she was.

We stayed with them for the first week after coming home from the hospital to help with feeding, diapering, rocking, and hugging our tiny granddaughter who has increased our joy in immeasurable ways.

And to this day, each time I embrace sweet Angela, I think of Mom, who loved babies . . . and hugs.

Maddie's Birthday Surprise

*T*oday is my birthday!

It was the first thing Maddie thought when she opened her eyes.

"Hooray! I'm five," she said to her cat, Snickers, who lay sleeping on her bed. "Today is my birthday. Hooray."

Snickers stretched and yawned and went back to sleep.

The second thing Maddie thought was, *I guess cats just don't understand about birthdays.*

The third thing she thought was that there were pretty packages in the living room. First, one had appeared. Then another. Then another. Maddie *really* wanted to know what was inside.

"No peeking until your birthday," Mommy had said. But Maddie still liked to look at the shiny paper with pictures of fairies and dancers and balloons.

The next thing Maddie thought was about getting out of bed and running into Mommy and Daddy's room. But the sun wasn't up yet. Only the light from the lamppost by the street came through her window.

Then Maddie thought about the rules. Don't bother Mommy or Daddy until the sun is up—unless it's something *really* important, like being sick or having a bad dream. Until then, she had to stay in her room and look at her books or play with her toys or play with Snickers.

Maddie tickled Snickers under her chin, but Snickers did not want to play.

Maddie got out of bed and pulled out a book. She loved her books—especially the one about the playful puppy—but it was too dark to see the colors in the pictures.

Maddie looked at her toys. Except for Mr. Buster, her favoritest teddy bear, they were little-kid toys. Toys a four-year-old would play with. She needed a toy for a big girl who was five.

"I wonder if any of those pretty packages in the living room has a toy for a five-year-old," Maddie said.

"Why don't you go and find out?" Mr. Buster said.

Maddie picked up Mr. Buster and looked at him, straight in his shiny black eyes. She was surprised he would suggest such a thing. "You know the rules, Mr. Buster," Maddie said, shaking her finger at his nose. "No peeking at presents."

"But you're already five," Mr. Buster said. "It's your birthday. Why can't you open your presents now?"

Maddie frowned. She had waited, with no peeking, until her birthday, just as Mommy had said she should. Could Mr. Buster be right? Would it be okay to peek, now that it was her birthday?

Usually, Maddie would ask her parents a question like this. But they were asleep, and Maddie didn't think this was quite as important as being sick or having a bad dream.

Maddie wasn't sure what to do, so she took Mr. Buster over to her bed and asked Snickers.

"Do you think it would be okay to peek at my presents now?" she said to the napping cat. "It *is* my birthday, after all."

Snickers opened one eye. "Nope," she said in a sleepy voice and closed her eye.

Maddie sat on the bed next to Snickers. Deep down inside, she agreed with her cat.

"But *why?*" Mr. Buster asked. "As far as I know, there's no rule about not opening your presents *on* your birthday."

Then Maddie thought about the rules. Don't run with scissors. Don't talk with your mouth full. Say "please" and "thank you." No hitting. No biting. No drawing on anything except paper. There were *so many* rules. But she couldn't remember one that said you couldn't open your presents on your birthday.

"*Maybe* it's okay," Maddie said.

Snickers rolled over. "Can't a cat get any sleep around here?"

Maddie giggled. "Daddy says all you do is eat and sleep."

Snickers grumbled. "Mr. Buster is wrong. You need to wait until Mommy and Daddy are up. They will want to be there to give you your presents. Believe me. I know."

"How could *you* know such a thing?" Mr. Buster said. "You're just a cat."

"And you're just a bag of stuffing," Snickers said. Maddie hated it when they argued.

"Besides," Snickers continued, "remember my last birthday? Mommy and Daddy wrapped up a catnip mouse and put it on the kitchen counter."

"I remember that," said Maddie. "You could smell it from the floor, and really wanted to open it."

"Mommy hadn't said 'no peeking,' so I stretched up to see if I could bat it off the counter with my paw."

Maddie nodded. "But you couldn't reach it."

"True. I could have jumped up on the counter to get it, but there's a rule about being on the kitchen counter. There are *so many* rules."

"You can say that again," said Mr. Buster.

Snickers twitched her whiskers. Maddie knew she was thinking about mentioning the rule about not interrupting, but was glad when Snickers just went on with her story.

"*Anyway*," Snickers said, "later in the day, Mommy and Daddy not only gave me the catnip mouse but lots of very satisfying strokes as well." Snickers half-closed her eyes just thinking about them. "It made me extra happy. Much happier than if I had opened it by myself. And I think it made them extra happy, too, just because they were there when I opened it."

"I like making Mommy and Daddy happy," Maddie said.

"I hadn't thought of that," Mr. Buster admitted. "Perhaps the cat is right."

"Okay," Maddie said. "I'll wait. But what should I do until Mommy and Daddy get up?" She lay on her bed, holding Mr. Buster, waiting for an idea to come to her.

* * *

"Good morning, birthday girl." Mommy kissed Maddie's forehead.

"Such a sleepy head on such a special day," Daddy said, tickling Maddie. "It's time to get up and open your presents."

Maddie opened her eyes. Bright sunlight came through her bedroom window. The first thing she thought was, *The sun is up. Today is my birthday. Hooray! I'm five.*

Daddy scooped her up out of bed. Snickers jumped down and ran ahead of them as Daddy carried Maddie out of her room. Mommy picked up Mr. Buster and brought him along to the living room where Maddie's presents waited, wrapped in shiny paper.

"Happy birthday, Maddie," Mommy and Daddy said. Then they sang her the "Happy Birthday" song.

Maddie reached up and gave big, birthday-girl hugs to her parents. She was surprised at how extra happy she felt. Her parents' big smiles told her they were extra happy, too.

Maddie looked at Mr. Buster, who winked a shiny black eye. Then she turned to Snickers, who nodded her head and twitched her whiskers.

The next thing Maddie thought was, *I guess cats do understand about birthdays after all.*

Connecting the Dots

Shut up in a dusty attic was about the last place I wanted to be on the first really sunny Saturday of the Spring. But how could I say no?

"Dory, dear," my mom said when she called. "I need your help."

I knew when she added "dear" to my name she was making an offer I couldn't refuse.

"I'll be over around ten, Doe," I said, using the nickname everyone called her, including us kids.

"And bring some trash bags," she added as I hung up the phone.

I had hoped to get outside and enjoy the sunshine, but Doe had something else in mind.

I was the only one of my mom's six kids who had not completely left the nest, so to speak. The others had gone off to various colleges, married people from far away, and established careers in other states. But my parents divorced in my last year of high school, so I lived at home and went to the local community college.

Oh—don't get me wrong; I don't still live at home. I moved last year, when I was twenty-five, to share a townhouse with two of my friends from high school. But I was still the one who lived in town—and still the one that she called when she needed help with anything.

When I arrived that morning, Doe was at least a little apologetic. "Thank you, sweetheart. I know it's not what you'd like to be doing, but I have the get the house ready to—"

She couldn't finish the sentence. Doe had grown up in that house. It belonged to her grandparents, for heaven's sake. She loved every square inch—creaky floors, noisy pipes, and drafty windows included. But now she had to sell because, in a fit of matrimonial optimism, she put my dad's name on the deed. Now he wanted "his share" of the money out of it. No way my mom could buy him out, so she had to sell her family legacy and the only place she—or I—had ever really called home.

"It's just that . . ." she continued, steadying her voice, "I feel like losing this house is like losing my mother and grandmother all over again."

It made me sick to think about it. Each of us kids had taken a crack at Dad, trying to get him to change his mind. "Financial reverses" was his only answer. He needed the money.

So today, I was going to go up into the attic to try to cull the must-keeps from the why-did-we-save-*theses*. I figured that there would be a lot more of the latter.

Truth be told, I thought it might be fun. You know—find an old item tucked away by great-grandma that would bring tens of thousands on *Antiques Roadshow*? I mean, my family was never rich, but *geez*—they had to have *something* worth keeping to have filled up an entire attic, right? If I could find it, Doe could stay.

So, armed with a cold bottle of water and a fresh box of trash bags, I picked my way up the cluttered staircase. Everything from hub caps to metal milk jugs blocked the path, daring me to make my way to the top. When I got there, I was pleased that I could stand upright—at least down the center of the space.

Any thoughts I had of an authentic Tiffany lamp or Chippendale bureau or long-lost Vermeer died when I saw the stacks of dusty trunks and sagging boxes stacked willy-nilly under the sloping rafters. They nearly obliterated the meager light that came through the smudged-up windows at the gable ends. Fortunately, despite a collection of dented oil lamps, somewhere along the line someone ran electricity up here, so I had a bare bulb to see by—probably one of Edison's first.

A-a-a-a-CHOO! I never was too good with dust and this place was musty enough to give the Statue of Liberty asthma.

I unscrewed the cap of the water bottle and took a swig. *Okay,* I told myself. *It might be no picnic for you, but it's better than having Doe do it.* It made me feel a bit noble, and helped me get down to it.

By noon, I had gone through enough boxes to begin sorting them by type: cardboard boxes full of disintegrating newspapers (most of which had become mouse condos, sad to say); books and magazines from who knows how long ago that were growing a mold of some sort; and broken stuff. And by broken stuff, I mean all kinds: chairs with loose legs, a rocking horse with broken springs (and peeling paint that *had* to have lead in it), TVs in need of tubes they stopped making during the Nixon Administration; tools with broken handles; and a host of discarded toasters, lamps, blenders, shoe-shine machines, electric frying pans, and some things that I'm not really sure *what* they were. Beyond those was the most special category of all: stray pieces of stuff. I swear, my ancestors never threw anything out. If there was any chance that a screw, bolt, fitting, pipe, board, or twist-tie could be used again, it was preserved. It was then I realized this wasn't my mother's attic; it was junk heaven.

When Doe called up to see if I wanted lunch, I was glad to get back downstairs where I could inhale air I couldn't see. I'd check with her to see if we could get a dumpster delivered—and position it right below the attic window.

"Oh, Dory, you have cobwebs in your hair," she said, picking at the *schmutz* that had made me prematurely gray.

"That's the least of it," I said, rolling my eyes for effect. Then I saw her expression. It wasn't just sadness I saw there; it was grief. This was harder on her than she wanted to let on—even to me.

As I munched my turkey sandwich with mayo and cream cheese—don't knock it until you try it—I thought about what clearing out the attic meant to her. To me it was junk; to Doe it was her family—her whole life.

I *had* to find something of value that she could sell and buy Dad's share of the house.

* * *

I started in after lunch with renewed enthusiasm—and my iPad. Anything that looked like it might have intrinsic value got Googled. I didn't want to be one of those fools who let a priceless *whatever* get sold at a yard sale for two dollars.

But the more I dug through piles and boxes, the less optimistic I became. Even in mint condition, the antiques I found were pretty common and not worth much. And the stuff in this attic was seldom in mint condition. But I was determined to keep looking.

* * *

By Sunday night, I had looked into every box, moved every pile, and dug through every stack of odds and ends. Nothing. No treasure that would enable Doe to keep the house.

There was just one trunk left to open. From the size of it, I knew it wouldn't hold anything large. What could possibly fit in there that would be valuable enough to save her home? Coins? Jewelry? My people weren't the kind to have a treasure horde. Could an antique clock or lamp of sufficient value be locked inside? Only one way to find out.

I wiped my dirty hands on my jeans. There was a padlock on the trunk, but no key. I had been finding loose keys for two days. *Where did I put them?*

I found the bin I'd used to hold small items that might be of some use and dug through. I found old skeleton keys, car keys, house keys, and luggage keys. There were only five keys, though, that might fit the padlock on the trunk. I tried the first. No—of course it wasn't the one. In such situations, you always need to try all five before you find the correct one, right? That is, if you actually have the correct one at all. So, I tried the second. It jiggled just a little in the lock. My heart skipped a beat.

"Where is that WD-40?" I asked aloud, looking around. I found the can and shook it up, hoping the propellant would still work. I popped the cap and sprayed the snot out of that lock.

I inserted the key again. It wiggled a little more than before. I knelt next to the trunk, leaned against the lid, and bore down with all the force my tired fingers could manage.

It opened. *It opened!*

I removed the lock from the hasp and undid the latches. I was almost afraid to lift the lid. This was my last chance to be a heroine.

I yanked it open.

Paper. That stupid trunk was filled with stacks of notebooks and loose paper. I knew that unless one of them was a copy of the *Magna Carta*, Doe was screwed.

I took out one of the broken chairs. With a couple of screws from the loose junk box, I was able to make it stable enough for my purposes. Then I pulled out an old floor lamp with frayed wiring. I was sure I had seen . . . Sure enough, there was lamp cord in the perhaps-salvageable box. I was able to make a quick job of rewiring it and plugging it into the lone outlet under the window. I turned the switch, and—no—of course the old light bulb had blown. But there was a box of incandescent bulbs somewhere around here, too. In a few moments—light! A lot of it. It must have been a hundred-watt bulb. So I dug around until I found an old, maroon, chenille lampshade, complete with frayed ball fringe on the bottom. Hideous, but utilitarian.

I pulled the lamp over to the chair and picked up the first few sheets. There was cursive writing all over it—a bit flowery—in what now looked like light brown ink. *Must be old. Oh, could I at least find a treasure map?*

* * *

"What is it?" Doe asked. My Cheshire-cat grin and hands held behind my back must have alerted her to my excitement at my discovery.

"Sit down," I said, keeping my treasure behind me to prevent her getting a look at what I was concealing.

She sat on the chintz sofa, and I moved to sit next to her, but she put up an arm. "No you don't, sister. Not in those dirty pants. Get a towel before you sit on my sofa."

I obeyed, and, when I was finally next to her, said, "Now close your eyes and hold out your hands." She looked at me sideways but did as I asked.

"What did you find?" she asked. "You're being very mysterious."

"These," I said, placing a stack of small books into her hands.

She opened her eyes and held the stack up close to her face. I knew the musty smell of those old books was a little off-putting, but it wasn't the smell that made me bring them down to her.

"What are these?" I think she hoped I found first editions of Shakespeare's folios, but, of course, my people wouldn't have those, either.

"They're diaries," I said, trying to keep the triumph out of my voice.

"Diaries? Whose?" Doe put the stack in her lap and picked up the top volume, opening it to the fly leaf. She gasped. "Dorothea. Why she . . . she's my great-great-grandmother!"

"Yes! And some from her daughter, and even a few from her granddaughter."

"Where were they? I never knew they were there. I didn't think we had any papers of Dorothea's. Just the old stories handed down."

"I know. I've heard them all my life. How she came to the US after the Civil War with nothing but the goods she could carry and a two-year-old daughter in hand."

"That child was my great-grandmother, Thea," Doe said nodding. "Dorothea started a dressmaking business and built it up to be one of the most successful in the city." She had a far-off look in her eye. "But none of her work survived except that pillow I've saved for you."

"There are some of Dorothea's patterns up there, too."

Her eyes grew wide. "I almost thought the whole story was just a family legend."

"And in each generation since, a daughter has been named 'Dorothea' in her honor," I said. "Me, you, Grandma Dot, Great-grandma Dottie, and Thea. It's a long chain," I said, feeling like I was part of something big and important.

She put her hand against my cheek. "I almost broke that chain. I didn't give the name to either of your sisters, but somehow, when you were born, it just seemed like I'd been saving it for you all along."

"*Awww*," I said, giving her a hug. We both blinked back tears for a moment. Then I remembered I had something else to show her. "That's not all," I said, flourishing a photo in a metal frame from behind my back, magician-style. "We have her picture." I held up the image of a young woman, dressed in all black—Victorian widow's weeds—with a young girl at her side. On the bottom, their names were written in what I now knew to be Dorothea's handwriting, and the date: 1872.

Now the tears really flowed. "I never saw a photo of her," Doe said. "Even without their names, I'd know that the little girl must be Thea. I only knew her as a *very* old woman, but I can see the determined expression in her eyes."

I scrutinized the child's face, trying to make it look like Doe or me or Grandma Dot. "I don't see a resemblance," I said.

Doe pursed her lips. "Perhaps not," she said, but then turned to me with an arched brow. "But surely you can see something else?"

I studied the photo in a way I hadn't when I found it in the attic. It was a typical late-1800s photo—stiff bodies, unsmiling faces. The clothes were typical of the age. But then I studied Dorothea's face. "She looks kind of familiar," I said.

"Oh, Dory," Doe said. "She's you!"

* * *

I never found a treasure that would save Doe's house. She sold it and paid cash for a condo with her share. But what I did find enabled Doe to take our family with her. It was worth much more than an old house with creaky floor boards, noisy pipes, and drafty windows.

I found a connection to our ancestors—and an even stronger connection to my mom.

The Man from Hooverville

Mother always had something to give the men who came to the back door. Their threadbare clothing and care-worn countenance told her all she needed to know. They never had to tell her their story of losing a job or a home or a family. She just put a finger to her lips and invited them to have a seat on the bench on the back porch. Moments later, she brought them a bit of whatever leftovers we might have, or what she was preparing for our dinner. The Depression had hit everyone hard, she said, and they deserved to have their dignity. "There but for the grace of God . . ."

So, one warm Monday in late April, when a young-looking man rapped on our back door while Mother was at work, I didn't hesitate to follow her example. This gentleman was different from the rest. His suit looked new, and his shirt was bright white. He was clean shaven, not scruffy like some who came to our door.

And, instead of a woebegone expression, he had a quick, friendly smile. He hadn't been on the road long, I guessed. He still had hope.

"Hi there," he said, tipping his hat when I answered his shave-and-a-haircut knock. At first, I thought he might be a salesman, but they usually came to the front.

"I'll get you something to eat," I answered, keeping the closed screen door between us. "Just sit over there."

"Actually," he said, arching one brow, "I was wondering if you folks have any work you need to have done around here. I see your lawn could use a mowing, and I'd be happy to fix that loose railing on the porch here. I could even add a coat of paint on your shed. Looks like it could use it."

I scowled, realizing he was right. Even though we lived in Minnesota, the lawn already had a shaggy spring growth. And I had to admit the porch railing was a bit loose and the shed looked pretty neglected. But did he really need to point out all the ways Mother and I hadn't managed to maintain our home the way Daddy would have?

He came closer to the door and looked directly into my eyes. "I'd be happy to help you get started with some of the work around here."

I wasn't stupid. I understood that young ladies needed to be cautious, and I knew better than to give him a reason to hang around. He seemed nice, but you could never tell.

"I'd be happy to give you something to eat, but I don't think we need any work done. We have it under control."

"Under control" was Mother's favorite phrase these days. It seemed to me that since Daddy died, we couldn't control anything anymore. But she pretended we could, and I went along.

While Daddy was alive, the three of us made out okay. Mother stayed at home, I went to school, and Daddy worked as an accountant at whatever jobs he could piece together. We were never rich, but we did okay.

After cancer took Daddy late last winter, Mother found office work and, at fourteen, I was able to chip in babysitting money. We could stay in our little house—for the present, at least. We were so much better off than many. Certainly better off than this man, and all the others who lived in the Hooverville shanty town down by the railroad tracks. It was named in honor of President Hoover who got us into this Not-So-Great Depression. I never thought I would talk to someone who lived there. Everyone said they were all hobos and thieves.

The man looked disappointed when I told him we didn't need help, so I hurried to add, "I think we have some bread, and maybe a bit of left-over chicken in the icebox."

He smiled again. Suddenly that didn't seem like enough of a meal. "And maybe part of an orange," I added.

"That's more than generous, Miss," he said, reaching for the screen door handle. "And, if it's not too much trouble, maybe a glass of cold water?"

I hooked the screen door lock, and he took a step back. "Have a seat on the bench," I said, following Mother's routine. "I'll be right back."

I sliced some bread and checked the ice box. I knew Mother was counting on the chicken for tonight's casserole but was sure she would want me to share with the less fortunate. I hesitated as I approached the screen door. What if this man . . .? No—he didn't seem scary. In fact, something about him seemed . . . familiar.

I undid the hook with one knuckle and opened the screen door with my hip as I balanced the food and water glass. He stood at one end of the bench as I brought it out.

"Thank you most kindly, Miss," he said. "Won't you join me, perhaps for a little conversation?" He patted the other end of the bench.

"No," I said, "I was in the middle of something. Just leave the dishes there when you're done." I opened the screen door and stepped inside. "And good luck to you," I said as I hooked the lock and closed the inner door.

I watched for a moment from the kitchen window, my heart pounding, not sure what to think of this man. But remembering Mother's insistence on allowing such men their dignity, I left the kitchen and settled on the davenport in the living room to start my homework. *Doing well in school is your most important job.*

Mother's voice ran through my head. I had to work hard to get the diploma Mother missed out on.

The city sounds of cars and children and distant sirens wafted into the room, but I focused on my mathematics, nearly forgetting the man on the porch. As the room began to darken, I got up to turn on the light. Mother would be home soon; it was time to start preparing dinner. My culinary skills were modest, but I was learning.

Crossing the kitchen, I opened the back door. The plate, flatware, and water glass were stacked neatly on the bench, but there was no sign of the man. He'd even disposed of the chicken bone. I stepped outside to retrieve the dishes, but just as I was about to pick them up, a thought struck me. I went over to the porch steps and wiggled the railing. It was looser than I'd realized.

***

When Mother came home, she was exhausted. Riding the streetcar to and from work, and making two transfers each way, made her work day very long. I served her the casserole I had made with what was left of the chicken.

"Seems kind of light on meat," she said, poking it with her fork. "I'm sorry, Patty."

"Oh—it's my fault. A man came to the back porch, and I gave him the leg."

Mother stopped eating. "While you were here alone?"

I nodded.

"I'm not sure that was a good idea, sweetie," she said, shaking her head and fixing me with a stern gaze. "Perhaps you shouldn't open the door when you're home alone."

We hadn't yet worked out all the rules for our new life without Daddy, but I could feel irritation rise within me. I was careful, and everything turned out all right.

I took a deep breath before responding, "I did just as you always do," I said. "I had him sit on the bench while I put together a plate of bread and chicken and some orange segments. Oh—and I gave him a glass of water from the pitcher in the icebox. Then I left him alone while he ate."

"Well, I think it's better if you keep the doors locked when you're in the house alone from now on," she said.

My jaw was set, which made it harder for me to chew—or to swallow her lack of confidence in my ability to handle things in her absence. I had to be able to handle things. She was taking as many hours at work as she could get, so I was alone at home every day after school and part of every Saturday. She would just have to get used to the fact that I wasn't a child.

But I decided she was right about locking the screen door.

***

The next day after school, I heard whistling outside. I went to the kitchen door, and there was the same man, dressed exactly the same, except that he had removed his hat and jacket. He stayed at the bottom of the porch steps and spread some tools on a cloth on the ground.

I hoped he didn't want more food. Our kitchen looked like Old Mother Hubbard's. All I could offer him was a thin slice of bread and a glass of water. Wasn't that what they gave prisoners?

I was supposed to go down to the market after I finished my homework. I had helped Mother make the shopping list: a pound of ground beef, a dozen eggs, a box of macaroni, a pound of cheese, a loaf of bread, some vegetables, and a quart of milk. We had saved nearly a whole dollar in the money jar, which should cover it, but it wouldn't help me feed the man now.

He looked up and saw me watching him. I waved half-heartedly through the screen. He smiled and bowed, before going to work on our loose railing. He narrated as he went.

"First thing we do is drill a hole on the bottom of the post into the stair below . . . " I watched everything he did and took notes. We had a loose banister inside the house, too. I used to like watching Daddy work with his tools, but he had never shown me how to use them. This man seemed happy to teach me.

As he finished and started putting his tools away, I realized I still hadn't come up with any ideas about how to feed him. I stuck my head in the icebox, wondering if adding pickles would make bread and water more of a meal. Then I heard his distinctive knock.

"Hi there," he said. "You're all fixed now." He smiled and gave a *ta-da* flourish. "Come and see what quality work I do. You can recommend me to your friends."

I hesitated, but it wasn't like I hadn't been outside with him before.

I opened the screen door and walked across the porch.

"Try it. It won't bite."

I tried to wiggle the railing, but it was solid.

"Wow," I said. "Great work."

He looked me in the eye and said, "Once you learn how to use tools like this, there is nothing you can't fix."

I blushed a little. "I don't know how to thank you." I really didn't. I couldn't pay him, and I couldn't really feed him.

"You just did," he said. "This is my way of thanking you for your generosity yesterday."

"I'm sorry, but I don't have any food in the house except some bread . . . and water."

He laughed. "Isn't that what they give prisoners?"

I could feel my face get warm and knew I was turning bright red. I hated blushing. I tried to laugh in a poised, movie-star fashion, but felt like an idiot. I had to change the subject.

"Where did you get the tools?" I asked, hoping he might not be homeless after all.

"Some nice fella where I'm staying loaned them to me. He was once quite a carpenter."

"Oh, well, thank your friend for me, too, okay?" I backed up toward the door.

"I certainly will," he said, putting on his jacket and tipping his hat before placing it on his head. "It's been a pleasure, Miss . . . ?"

He wanted to know my name. Well, what was the harm? He already knew where I lived.

"Shephard." There. I'd said it. But I wouldn't tell him my first name.

"Well then, it's been a pleasure, Miss Shephard."

He gathered the tools and strode away, whistling a song I almost recognized. I guessed he didn't want bread and water after all.

As he walked toward the street, I called after him. "Wait! What's your name?"

Without turning, he called back, "Just call me Joe." Then he whistled his way down the street.

***

After school on Wednesday, I hoped Joe might return, but even after I finished my homework, there was still no sign of him. It was too soon to start dinner, but the grass still need-ed mowing. Mother mowed it last fall after Dad-dy got sick, but she hadn't pulled the mower out yet this spring. These days, she came home so tired. She wouldn't be able to get to it until Saturday, and by then it would have grown even longer.

Daddy's old mower was in the shed. I had watched him oil it around the rubber wheels and sharpen the curved blades, but he never showed me how. It wasn't women's work, he said. Except now it was.

I pulled the mower out of the shed and hoped it would work without having to oil it or sharpen it. But it had been many months since we last used it.

I tilted the mower and rolled it over to the grass, lined it up, and pushed. It didn't budge. I stepped back and leaned with all my might against the handle. The mower crept forward, slowly at first, then more easily. Soon the familiar rattle of the blades reminded me of summer. I could almost close my eyes and imagine Daddy mowing, and me making lemonade for him to drink when he was done.

I mowed a long, wobbly swath from the shed to the house. Daddy always said, when you have a big job to do, don't look at how much is left to finish—look at all the progress you've made so far. So, I turned back to see what I'd accomplished.

I could clearly see where I had passed the mower over the grass—not because it was neatly clipped, but because the long grass just lay on the ground, bent flat by the mower. Only a bit of grass had made it to the blades and left their shorn tops on my shoes and socks. I wanted to cry. How did Mother do it? Why hadn't Daddy shown me how?

I heard a familiar whistle coming from up the street. I left the mower and scrambled into the house, locking the screen door. I was still in the kitchen when I heard his knock.

I smoothed my hair before I answered the door.

"Hi there, Miss Shephard. I see you agree with me that the lawn could use a mowing," he said. "Shall I help you?" He rolled up his white sleeves revealing tanned arms. "Your roller is probably set at the wrong height, and your mower might need a bit of sharpening. I'd be happy to help."

"No need," I said. I'm not sure why, but I didn't want him in Daddy's shed.

"It's no trouble at all," he said, striding over to the mower. I opened the door and followed him.

He brushed off the grass clippings, and checked the blades, just as I'd seen Daddy do. "Here. Let me show you how."

I almost said no. I almost told him to leave Daddy's things alone. But this man had already been helpful, and if he could teach me how to use the mower, it would make things easier for Mother.

"You see," he began, "here's how you adjust the roller. . . ."

Before I knew it, I had helped him sharpen the mower blades, and cut some of the grass.

"I'll take it from here," he said. "Why don't you go get dinner started for your mother."

I glanced at my watch. He was right; I needed to start dinner. When I set the table, I almost pulled out a third plate, like I always did when Daddy was with us. The memory made me choke up, but I didn't want to cry. Not with the man just outside.

I heard the mowing stop. I didn't have any lemons to make lemonade, but the least I could do was offer him a glass of water. I chipped some ice from the shrinking block in the ice box into a glass. It wasn't lemonade, but it would have to do.

"Ice water," he said. "Thank you kindly, Miss Shephard." He turned to sit on the bench.

"The ice man will come tomorrow, so . . ."

"It's a luxury, and I am grateful," he said, finishing the glass and standing to go.

"Oh, uh, dinner will be ready in about half an hour if you can wait."

He looked up at the sky and shook his head. "Thank you, but your mother will be home soon, and you'll be able to show her all you've done today. I would only be in the way." He tipped his hat and descended the steps. I could still hear his whistle long after he disappeared around the corner of the house.

***

Mother was impressed with the cut grass and ready dinner. She seemed in a better mood than usual, so I didn't let on that I had gone out-side and let Joe show me how to mow the lawn. After dinner, we played cards and listened to *One Man's Family* on the radio before I had to go to bed.

That night, I dreamt that Daddy was alive. He looked like he did before he got so thin and sickly. His shiny head with a fringe of graying hair reflected light from a bright sun, and his mustachioed face held its usual broad grin. I ran to him, saying, "I'm so glad you're alive. I thought you were supposed to be dead."

Behind his glasses, he arched one eyebrow higher than the other. When I was younger, I spent a lot of time teaching myself to do just that. Then he said, "I know I'm supposed to be dead, but that doesn't mean I can't come back to visit you, Patty-Girl." I leaned into him and felt the warmth of his hug. "I'm sorry I didn't prepare you better . . . ," he said. Then I awoke in the darkness. Daddy was gone. The hole he left in my heart ached, and I cried myself back to sleep.

***

It rained all day Thursday. Before I left for school, I remembered to put the cardboard ICE sign in the front window. I only felt a little guilty about chipping some of the last of our ice block into Joe's water glass the day before. Mother probably would have wanted ice today anyway.

I grabbed my umbrella and left for school, knowing the ice man could get the new block of ice into the icebox through the little door on the porch.

The gray weather matched my mood. I was really missing Daddy, especially during math. Daddy was always so good with numbers. I used to watch him run his finger down a long string of digits, adding them in his head. Being an accountant, he had an adding machine, but he said his head was faster and more accurate because he never hit the wrong button in his brain. "Max," people used to say, using his first name, "you're a numbers whiz." I wished my brain could do that.

It was still raining when I walked home from school. I avoided puddles and dodged waves of dirty water splashed up by passing cars, but my feet got wet despite my best efforts, turning the scuffed toes of my saddle shoes dark. I would have to polish them when they dried.

As I approached our house, I looked for Joe. He wasn't in the yard or on the back porch, and I couldn't hear him whistling down the street. The rain probably kept him back at the Hooverville where I'd heard they burned fires in old metal drums to keep the chill off. I couldn't blame him.

I curled up on the davenport, threw Mother's knitted afghan over my knees, and started on my homework, but I just couldn't concentrate.

I knew Daddy kept his tools in a metal box in the shed, so I went out through the rain and brought it inside. Opening it, I looked at each tool. Daddy's hands were the last ones to touch the drill, but now I had to. Could I really use it by myself?

I got out the notes I took when Joe was fixing the porch rail and found everything I needed. Putting aside my doubts, I went to work.

I loved turning the drill handle and seeing the curls of wood spin out. But I remembered to keep the drill straight, just as Joe said. Slowly, I mimicked what I remembered Joe doing on Tuesday.

It took me a lot longer than it took him, but when I was done, the banister didn't wobble anymore. I'd done it! All by myself. I wished Daddy were there to see it—or even Joe.

Instead of putting the toolkit back in the shed, I stowed it under my bed. They were my tools now, and thanks to Joe, I knew how to use them. I couldn't wait for him to show me more—if he ever came back. I'd heard most Hooverville folks moved around a lot. When there was no work for them in one place, they'd get on a train and go someplace else.

When Mother came home, I hadn't even started getting dinner ready. She didn't scold me, but I could see the disappointment in her eyes.

"Did your homework take you all afternoon to finish?" she asked, putting down her purse and pulling out her hat pin.

"Well . . ." I tried hard to conceal my smile. "I didn't get it done yet."

"They really shouldn't assign so much that you can't finish it before dinner." She went into the kitchen and pulled out a saucepan to make her famous macaroni and cheese. I set the table and settled down with my homework to await dinner. I knew Mother wouldn't notice the banister until she was ready to go upstairs, but I couldn't wait for bedtime.

"Wait," I said before she could even boil the macaroni. "Come and see what I did."

I brought her over to the banister. "Wiggle it," I said. She reached out and took hold of the newel post. Despite her effort, it stood stock-still.

"What did you do?" she asked, looking surprised. "This used to be so loose."

"I fixed it . . . using Daddy's tools," I said, beaming. "The man from Hooverville fixed the one on the back porch, and I watched him as he worked. Then I did this one myself."

"Patty, are you sure you didn't let the man into the house to do it for you?"

I was hurt. Not only did Mother think I couldn't do the work on my own, but worse, she didn't trust me to tell her the truth.

***

By Friday afternoon, the rain had dried up, and the sun was warm, promising the coming days of summer. As I walked home from school, I remembered Mother's accusation. I had shown her my notes, and Daddy's tools under my bed. I think she finally believed me, but I still felt bad about the whole thing.

Then I thought about how much Joe had taught me. He was like a big brother, and I wished, not for the first time, that I wasn't an only child.

No sooner had I formed the thought than I heard footsteps and turned to see Joe striding up next to me.

"Where did you come from?" I was so startled; I hadn't been aware of his approach.

"Where I always come from," he said. I guessed he didn't want to admit he lived in the Hooverville, so I let it go at that.

His clothes were still clean. I was surprised because I got grass stains on my socks on Tuesday and working on the banister made me perspire. Did he have changes of clothes in his Hooverville shanty? I didn't think hobos had extra clothes.

"Where are you headed?" I asked, shifting my books in my arms. He reached out, offering to carry them for me, and I was happy to relinquish them.

"I thought perhaps we could start work on that shed of yours this afternoon." He looked up at the clear sky. "The wood won't be dry enough for paint until tomorrow, but today, we can get everything ready. Do you know if you have any spare paint in the shed?"

"I *think* so," I said, hurrying my pace to keep up with his long strides. "We can check when we get there."

As we arrived at the house, Joe dropped my books on the back porch and went straight to the shed.

"I have to change my clothes," I said, going inside . . . and locking the door. By the time I emerged, he was using a stiff brush to scrub the clapboard walls. "You have to get all the loose dirt and paint off first," he said, narrating as he went along. "And scuff up the shiny surface of the last coat of paint so the new paint will stick." We tied back the early stalks of Mother's peonies so they wouldn't touch the newly painted surface. Joe showed me how to nail in a couple of loose boards and cover the hardware with tape to keep it from getting painted over. Together we checked Daddy's paint cans and brushes to see if we had what we needed.

"Looks good," he said after we finished. "I'll be back tomorrow. Now you'd better get dinner started." He left, whistling his usual tune before I could even suggest warming up some leftovers.

Tomorrow. I worried what Mother would think when she saw Joe there. She wasn't happy that I was letting him help us out around the yard—and she didn't yet know I was outside with him. Would she be angry? I knew she would. But since Mother would meet him, wouldn't she be certain to realize he was helpful, and not a threat at all? I hoped so.

***

Mother worked on Saturday morning, and soon after she left, Joe appeared. We worked together, painting with long, overlapping strokes along the wood grain until we completed the back and the far side of the shed. We finished in just over an hour and were about to start the front—where Mother would see it—when Joe said, "That's enough for me today."

"Why?" I asked. "Can't we finish it up and surprise my mother?"

Joe just shook his head. "Got to be on my way. Besides," he said, looking me straight in the eye, "you can take it from here." Then he winked.

Before he left, he showed me how to clean his brushes, then tipped his hat, and strode away, whistling that tune.

As I watched him go, I decided that I didn't want to wait until he returned to finish the shed, so instead of cleaning my brushes, I got back to work. It took a lot longer without Joe's help, but I finished half of the near side of the shed before Mother returned. As I'd hoped, she was very pleasantly surprised.

"What a wonderful thing for you to do," she exclaimed. "Whatever made you think of it?"

"That man from the Hooverville mentioned that it needed painting the first time he came."

Mother's smile froze. "Was he back today?"

I looked at my shoes. "Yes, Mother, but he's really nice. He knows how to fix things, and

I've learned so much from him. Without him, I couldn't have mowed the lawn or fixed the banister . . . or painted the shed."

Mother gave me a scowl that was almost half a smile. I knew she wasn't quite angry, but not quite happy, either. "Well, let me get changed, and I'll help you finish," she said, removing her hat.

"Okay. I'll keep going until you get back." I thought about Joe not changing his clothes, yet he didn't seem to get a spot of paint on his trousers. Despite the heat, he didn't seem to sweat, and his shirt was still the bright white it had been on the first day I saw him. *How did he manage that?* I wondered.

When Mother returned, I was just finishing work around the door—having masked the hinges with tape, just as Joe showed me. Mother picked up Joe's paintbrush and gave me a smile.

As we painted side-by-side, I started whistling. It wasn't something I did often. Mother used to say, "Whistling girls and cackling hens, always come to some bad ends." But I was happy, and whistling felt right.

Mother stopped painting and, in a scolding manner, asked, "What's that you're whistling?"

"It's just a tune the man from Hooverville whistles. I don't know what it is."

"Well I do," Mother said, obviously a little unhappy.

I wondered if it was a song not appropriate for girls my age. "Some bad ends," indeed. "What is it?" I asked, almost afraid to find out.

"It's an old song. Something from the Navy, I believe. Your father used to whistle it when I first met him."

"Daddy was in the Navy, wasn't he?"

"Yes. In the Great War."

"I don't remember Daddy ever whistling," I said. Then I realized, he probably stopped because Mother didn't like it. I stroked more paint on the wood and wondered if Joe were in the Navy. I was sure he was too young to have been in the Great War. "Sorry, I won't whistle it anymore," I said.

"It's okay," Mother said—a little sheepishly. "I like hearing that song again after all these years."

I hummed a bit, thinking of Daddy. When I pictured him, I still thought of how he looked when he was sick, thin, and weak. I wished I could remember him as he was before, with his mustache, wearing his glasses and a mischievous smile, and his bald head that I would kiss every night before going to bed. I wondered what he looked like when Mother first met him. In my mind's eye, I tried to imagine him young, with a full head of hair and clean shaven, whistling a tune, arching one brow. As his image came into focus, a shiver ran down my spine.

"Mother," I said, almost afraid of the answer. "Did people ever call Daddy any other name besides 'Max'?"

"Silly girl," Mother answered. "He's always been called 'Max.' It's his name."

I breathed a sigh.

Then, after a moment's hesitation, Mother said. "Except in the Navy when there were several people named Max in his squadron. Then they made up different nicknames for each of them. They called one 'Uncle,' and another one 'Sam.'" She chuckled at the memory of the joke before continuing. "But since they knew he was born in St. Joseph," she said, dipping her brush in the paint can, "they always called your daddy 'Joe.'"

My First Red Sox Game

Until age eight, my only experience with baseball was being dragged along to my big brother's games at Little League—an organization which, at that time, required all participants to have a Y chromosome. As "just a girl," I had to entertain myself during those seemingly endless, six-inning walk-a-thons, so I looked for four-leaf clovers, swatted mosquitoes, and killed time on a nearby swing set.

Then, in 1963, my grandmother moved into an apartment nearby. Suddenly I was spending a lot of my free time at Nana's place. That summer, she and I sipped lemonade in front of her oscillating fan and watched the Boston Red Sox on her black-and-white television. To my amazement, my Nana—*a girl*—was a baseball fan. She taught me how to keep a box score, making a chart out of notebook paper. Together we recorded each at bat, every hit or error, every score or strike out.

Nana was a kid when Fenway Park opened in 1912. In those days, the Red Sox were good. She even remembered when they last won the World Series in 1918. And she hoped, every year, that the Red Sox would win it all again. Her enthusiasm was infectious. Nana loved baseball, and I loved Nana.

I looked forward to every game at her place and was sad when the season ended. That year, Nana's team finished in seventh place in the American League, twenty-eight games behind those darn Yankees.

"That's okay," Nana said with a twinkle in her eye. "There is always next year."

By the following spring, I was eager for the season to start. I knew most of the stars: Carl Yastrzemski, Frank Malzone, Bob Tillman, and Felix Mantilla, but this year they added a new guy. Tony Conigliaro was a young "phe-nom." Soon he was hitting home runs like no other teenager in major league history. And it didn't hurt that he was kind of cute.

Then, one day, Nana asked me if I wanted to go to a game with her—in Boston. I said yes, almost before she finished the question. The date was set for early July—a game against the Minnesota Twins.

It took forever for the day to arrive. I dressed in my school clothes even though it was summer; Nana said we had to dress up to go into the city. She dressed up, too, but still wore her old Red Sox cap.

Nana didn't have a car, so we took the commuter train from West Concord to North Station. Then we got on the green line to ride to the park. The noisy, bone-shaking rumble and the smell of sweat and tobacco in the trolley added to the agitation in my stomach. We got off at Kenmore Square, and Nana helped me cross the street. Such a wide street and so many cars.

After a short walk, she pointed ahead of us.

"There it is," she said. "Fenway Park." I stared with my mouth open until she pulled at my hand, and we trudged on toward the stadium.

As we approached the gate, I couldn't wait to be inside watching Yastrzemski, Malzone, and of course, Tony C. I held tightly to Nana's elbow as she bought our tickets and navigated our way inside.

When we got into the park, I was amazed at how green everything was: the grass, the seats, and the huge green wall in left field. Having only seen Fenway Park on a black-and-white television, I hadn't expected it to be in color.

"I love this old park," Nana said, a smile on her face. "Babe Ruth played here, you know. He was a pitcher for the Sox in the old days."

I was surprised. I thought Babe Ruth was a Yankee.

We found our seats on the left field line, and I tried to get oriented. I had never seen the park from that angle before.

"Who's that?" I asked Nana, pointing to a big sign with a drawing of a boy in a wheelchair. The sign said, "I can *dream*, can't I?" Nana explained that the boy was named Jimmy. He was a baseball fan, but he had cancer.

"Some people started the Jimmy Fund to help him get a television in his hospital room so he could watch the games," she said. "Now it pays for research to cure cancer." I thought about Jimmy, and wondered if he were watching this game.

Soon my attention shifted to the many vendors hawking cotton candy, tonic, ice cream, and popcorn. Mom had told me that this was an expensive trip and Nana didn't have much money, so I should not ask her to buy me anything. I didn't ask, but I gave her my best smile as the popcorn man approached our row. She grinned and told me to close my eyes and hold out my hand. I did, and the next thing I knew she placed a quarter in my palm. I looked into her sparkling blue eyes and thanked her.

But a quarter wouldn't cover it. Popcorn was fifty cents. It came in a cardboard funnel, and when the popcorn was gone, you could pull a plug out of the narrow end, turning the funnel into a megaphone. I really wanted a megaphone. I tucked the quarter into my dress pocket, trying to figure out what to do.

The Red Sox took the field, and Nana and I took out our score sheets. Jack Lamabe was on the mound. Tony C. was playing in left. I waved and called, but he couldn't hear me. I needed one of those megaphones.

The first batter for the Twins, Versalles, hit a double. Then Rollins walked, filling first base. Tony Oliva, their star rookie, was next at bat. Lamabe got him swinging. I crossed my fingers for a double play—or at least a strike out. Lamabe pitched, Oliva swung the bat and connected for a three-run homer—with no outs.

Lamabe watched it go and dug his toe into the mound. *Don't let it get to you, Jack.* He picked up the rosin bag and threw it down as the Twins' clean-up batter, Harmon Killebrew, came to the plate. A quick single and he was on base. Next Allison, their center fielder, got a hit. Now there were two men on. Their first baseman, Mincher, came up and hit a long fly ball. It looked like it was going out, but Yaz caught it in deep center field. By the time it got back to the infield, two more runs scored—with only one out.

Lamabe was done. Bob Heffner replaced him on the mound and got us out of the inning, but after half an inning we were down 5-0.

That was okay; it was our turn to bat, and our boys did not disappoint us. They faced the Twins pitcher, Jim Kaat, and scored two runs in the bottom of the first, including a hit by Tony C. We were down by three, but we had eight more innings to catch up.

Heffner pitched solidly and shut them out in the second and the third. Unfortunately, Kaat shut us out, too. Then in the top of the fourth, the Twins scored again—only one run this time, but that put us down by four.

No one else scored until the top of the sixth. Heffner lost his stride, and the Twins pounded in six more runs. Fans were making noise, but instead of cheering for the Red Sox, they were yelling at them. I heard people call them the Boston Bums, or the Red Flops. I had to admit, that one was kind of funny.

A pitching change—we brought in Arnold Earley who got us out of the inning. But we were down 12-2.

Some Fenway fans started leaving as if the game were over, but Nana showed no signs of deserting her team. Two men in front of us stood and threw down their programs. Using a word whose meaning I did not know, they left— abandoning their popcorn funnels.

Careful to keep my skirt down, I climbed over the seats in front of us and grabbed one of the megaphones. I looked up at Nana, half expecting her to tell me to leave it there. Instead, she grinned.

"Can you hand me the other one?" she said. I giggled and passed it to her.

After I regained my seat, we took out the stoppers, and for the next half-inning we yelled our brains out. Fortunately for our vocal chords, it was a short inning. No score.

Earley kept the Twins' bats quiet in the top of the seventh inning. Then, in the middle of the seventh, everyone stood up and the organist played "Take Me Out to the Ball Game." I knew the words and sang along, but I was pretty sure I heard someone get the words wrong. It sounded like they sang, "Root, root, root for the Red Sox. If they don't win it's the same."

After the stretch, their pitcher started to tire. We scored three runs with the help of a pinch hitter for Earley and a home run by Mantilla. *Go Mantilla!*

We were down 12-5 with two innings to go.

Our new pitcher, Dave Gray, was not as good as Earley. The Twins got those three runs back in the top of the eighth.

The stands were nearly empty by the bottom of the eighth. Nana suggested we move down, closer to home plate. From there, we could see the expressions on the hitters' faces as they went up to bat. We brought our megaphones and cheered each one on. At one point, I swear, when Tony C. was on deck, he looked right at me and smiled. But he didn't get to bat. We finished the eighth inning down 15-5.

Gray shut the Twins out in the top of the ninth inning, but we still needed ten runs just to tie it up.

I was beginning to think the Sox were in trouble.

Conigliaro was up first. It was his fifth time at bat, and he already had two hits and a walk. Could he get a rally started?

There he was, at the plate, looking as if he were ready to slam at anything the pitcher threw him. The pitcher set, and threw. Conig hit a screaming grounder right past the short stop and out into center field. He was safe at first.

Next came Yastrzemski.

"This is the guy you want up in a situation like this," Nana said.

He waved his bat over his head like a weapon, and when the ball reached the plate, he hit it deep into the right field corner. Conigliaro scored from first, and Yaz had a stand-up triple.

The fans who were still there stood up, cheering. Nana and I screamed through our megaphones. If willpower alone could decide a game, the Sox would win this one for sure.

With the score at 15-6, Dick Stuart was up next. He'd had an off day, and this at bat went south for him fast. Three quick strikes and he headed for the dugout.

Dick Williams came in for Malzone. I stood there, crossing my fingers, my toes, my arms, and my legs. *Pu-leeze let him get a hit.*

The count went to 3 and 2. Williams fouled off one ball after another. *Okay—a walk will do. Just don't get an out.*

He finally saw a pitch he liked and powered it into the net over the left-field wall. Home run! Two more runs scored.

"Now we're only down by seven," I shouted to the entire stadium.

Next up was our right fielder, Lee Thomas. He walked, keeping the rally alive. Then came Eddie Bressoud, our short stop. He also walked, moving Thomas into scoring position.

We could win this!

Our catcher, Bob Tillman, came to bat. He'd had a tough day at the plate, but maybe, just maybe. . . . He hit a fly ball directly at the right fielder. Thomas tagged up and raced for third. Bressoud held at first. Two outs, with two men on.

It was time for our pitcher to bat. Did we dare bat Gray? Did we have any pitchers left in the bullpen for the tenth inning if we tied the game? The manager must have thought so because he sent in a pinch hitter named Chuck Schilling.

Ball one . . . strike one, foul . . . ball two . . . ball three. *A walk is as good as a hit—well, almost anyway.* Strike two—looking. Full count.

By now, almost no one in the stands had much of a voice left, but we managed to make noise anyway. I pounded my feet and banged the hollow megaphone on the back of the seat in front of me. *C'mon, Schilling.*

The pitcher looked in and nodded. The throw came in low, but Schilling dug it out for a single. Thomas raced home, and Bressoud got to third. We were down by six, with men at the corners, two outs, and the top of our order coming up.

Mantilla strode to the plate and took a few practice swings. The pitcher glared in at him. I hoped he was thinking about that homer in the seventh inning. The pitch came in. Foul ball, strike one. Mantilla was swinging for the fences but didn't hit it squarely. The next pitch was high; Mantilla chased it. Strike two.

C'mon Mantilla. You can do it.

The third pitch came in. Mantilla hit it hard and raced for first. I watched the ball rise toward left . . . and I saw it fall . . . into the fielder's glove.

Game over. Twins won 15-9.

The fans who were screaming only a moment before fell silent. The teams cleared the field. We collected our score sheets and megaphones and headed for the exit.

"Pitching. It all comes down to pitching," Nana muttered as we left. "A team that scores nine runs ought to win the ball game." She shook her head and looked at me. Then she took off her Red Sox cap and swatted me with it. "But did you have a good time, at least?"

"Are you kidding? It was great. I love this game." My smile felt like it would break my cheeks.

As we filed out of the stadium we heard the jingle of people with metal canisters, collecting for the Jimmy Fund. I remembered the quarter in my pocket and considered all the things I could buy with it. Then I thought about how much I loved watching baseball with Nana. I pulled out the quarter and put it in a can. I looked up at Nana, hoping she wouldn't mind that I spent it that way.

"So sick kids can watch baseball, too," I said.

Nana winked and put her arm around me. We might have lost the game, but we were happy because we were together.

***

The Red Sox finished that year in eighth place in the American League, twenty-seven games behind the Yankees. But Nana and I remained loyal fans, watching them together for the rest of her life. And forty years later, when they at last won the World Series again, my first thoughts were of her. *They finally did it, Nana.*

I have gone to many games in Fenway Park since that July day. Now tickets are costly, and nearly impossible to get. Young fans know only a world in which the Red Sox are contenders.

Still, for me, baseball will always be the game Nana introduced me to: the team you love whether it wins or loses, the park you love because of, not despite, its age, and the game you love because of who you're sharing it with.

And no matter who I'm with, I still share every game with Nana.

Summer Nights

With each step up the staircase, I feel the sweltering summer close in. Drawn shades during the day keep it tolerable downstairs, but Mom won't let us sleep on the couch. We'll never get any sleep upstairs. It's too hot.

Opening the window at the foot of my twin bed, I put my pillow against the footboard and hope for a puff of air. The metal screen, inches from my nose, taints the scent of warm pine. Cats do battle down the street, and moths circle the porch light.

Then the air stirs and forest branches sing me a lullaby.

Dark Side of the Light

When Joanne woke up, it was still dark. She rolled over. Sure enough, Eric still wasn't home. She would have been madder about him ruining her big announcement the evening before if she didn't have to rush to the bathroom with an urgent need to pee.

Before she got back under the covers, the nausea hit. The nurse said to keep some crackers on the nightstand to nibble first thing in the morning. She should get some at the store today. *At least nausea stops after the first trimester*. That was something, at least.

She closed her eyes for what she thought was just a moment or two, then awoke with a start when she realized Eric was there, sitting on the side of the bed in the gathering dawn with a weird smile on his face.

"Hey," she said, lifting herself up on her elbows. "You made it home."

"And I brought you something," Eric said, whipping a huge bundle of flowers from behind his back.

Guilt flowers, Joanne thought.

As if he could read her mind, Eric said, "They're an apology for all the hours I've been putting in at work lately."

She took the flowers and pressed them to her face. "Where did you get them at this hour? What time is it, anyway?"

"About quarter to six. I got them at the all-night grocer. Three bouquets. I spared no expense."

"I'd say you shouldn't have, but considering all the evenings you've left me alone, I'll accept them."

"Sorry, babe. Just a lot going on at work."

"Such as?" she asked, knowing that he couldn't and wouldn't say. Eric's work at NASA was classified, and he took its secrecy very seriously. "I mean," she continued, "it's not like you're about to send up a space shuttle or anything."

Eric worked with CNEOS at the JPL. She hated that the government used acronyms for everything. How was anyone supposed to know what they were doing? *Maybe,* she thought, *that's why they do it.*

"Oh, you know—with the eclipse and all. Hey—I saw the table still set for last night's dinner," he said, changing the subject. "It looks like you went to a lot of trouble. Really sorry, babe."

Joanne went from pleased to pissed. She *had* gone to a lot of trouble. Candles, champagne, her grandmother's good china, and Eric's favorite recipe—all for the big reveal. She had big news, and she wanted to tell him in just the right way.

At least Eric looked really sorry.

"I've decided to take the day off," he said.

"Not to sleep, I hope. If you sleep all day, you'll be jet-lagged for the rest of the week."

"Nah. I caught a cat nap in the lounge. I'm okay. I want to spend the whole day with you." He hesitated. "We can watch the eclipse together."

That will work out well, Joanne reasoned. *Now I'll have the whole day to figure out the best way to make my big announcement. Let me see . . .*

As he leaned in for a kiss, his phone chirped. He gave her a quick peck, checked his text, frowned, and stuffed the phone back in his pocket.

She thought about popping the champagne cork to make him a mimosa, and maybe eggs Benedict. *Ugh.* The thought of eggs sent her stomach roiling.

"C'mon," Eric said. "The sun is rising, and it's going to be another perfect day in Southern California out there." He coughed. "Let's make the most of it. We can do anything you want to do. Maybe something we've put off doing for a long time, and now have the perfect day to do it."

Yeah, Joanne thought. *I have just that kind of thing that I'm busy doing right now.* She grinned at her own cleverness.

"Okay—what's the joke?" Eric said, looking at her sideways.

"Aren't you tired?" she said, hoping to distract him from her grin.

"Sure, a little, but I've been neglecting you. Today, I'm all yours. I don't want to waste a minute of it."

"Well, I was going to do a little online shopping today," Joanne said, drawing out the words. Maybe he would browse with her, and once he saw what she was shopping for, she'd have a perfect way to break the news.

"Online shopping?" His shoulders slumped and he shook his head. Then he glanced up with a look of resolve. "Okay. If that's what will make you happy, feel free. And the sky's the limit. Spend anything you want—a one-day-only offer. Anything you want to order is fine with me."

"Okaaay," Joanne said, wondering what happened to her penny-pinching husband. "It really is what I want to do. Let's browse together."

"You go ahead. While you're shopping, I'll give my mom a call. It's later back East. Then after we're both done, we can do something together."

No, no. That's not the way this is supposed to work at all. But Eric had already pulled out his cell and pressed his mother's speed dial number. He walked away with his phone to his ear.

"But . . ." she called after him. He was gone. It was no use.

Joanne got dressed and looked in the mirror. Was she imagining it, or were her boobs a little rounder? *There ought to be some compensation for the soreness.* Except for the morning sickness with which she currently had a love/hate relationship, there was no obvious sign of pregnancy. Nothing to indicate that, after seven years of marriage, she and Eric were expecting a child.

When her cycle was late, she hadn't wanted to get his hopes up—especially with the long hours he'd been working. Even after the home test, she didn't dare tell him. But yesterday she had finally seen a doctor. She was eight weeks along, and she'd seen the tiny heartbeat on the ultrasound. She knew Eric would be over the moon when she told him. Everything had to be perfect.

She went to the kitchen to put the flowers in a vase. When Eric found her there, she looked up at him as brightly as she could.

"How's your mom?"

"Okay. I guess I woke her. I forget she sleeps in now that she's retired."

"You didn't talk long."

"No," he said. "I just told her that I loved her, and she said the same. Sends love to you as well."

Joanne rolled her eyes. "Sure she did." She knew she'd caught him in a lie. His mother had never taken a shine to her, and the years without producing grandchildren only cemented her dislike. But that didn't matter. Eric had chosen her. Enough said.

Eric took her in his arms. "Well, she would have sent her love if she had any idea how wonderful you are."

"Wow. Flowers and flattery. You ought to pull all-nighters more often if you come home all romantic."

She got the kiss she had been waiting for, and it gave her tingles from her lips to her bare feet.

"So what shall we do this morning?" she asked, pushing her sore breasts slightly away from his chest.

"I thought maybe we could go to the lake. Maybe rent a boat and do a little fishing, and watch the eclipse without a lot of trees in the way.

Fishing. That's his idea of a perfect day, not mine. She tried to imagine being out on the lake, in the hot sun, with the boat rocking. Nausea threatened again.

"It's what we did on our first date, remember?" he said.

"No," she said, punching him in the arm. "We went on a party boat at sunset with half the graduating class."

"Well, a bunch of us were fishing off the stern, and I remember a brown-eyed girl, who looked a lot like you, flirting with me."

She laughed. She was flirting. No reason to pretend otherwise. He was a hunk then, and had only improved with age—if your definition of hunk was a nerdy, bespectacled brainiac with a ready smile and a good sense of humor. *Yeah. Definitely a hunk. His kid is going to be as handsome as he is.*

His phone chirped again. He checked the text and frowned.

"Something wrong?"

"Nothing you need to worry about," Eric said, pocketing his cell and pasting on a smile. He stared at the wall for a moment. He seemed so intent on doing something memorable today.

He has no idea how memorable it's going to be, she thought, *if I can just figure out how to tell him. I hate keeping him in the dark.*

"Well, how about I take you out to an early breakfast, and we can figure it out from there," he said.

Her stomach felt a bit better. "Sure. Why not?"

***

On the way to their favorite diner, Eric kept looking at the sky. Joanne stared up through the tinted windshield, but couldn't guess what had captured his attention. So far, it was just a summer sky. The few clouds were high and thin, and the bright morning sun promised another hot day. The earth was parched from a mid-August dry spell, and the fire danger was high according to the sign outside the firehouse.

"The eclipse hasn't started, has it?"

"No, it won't . . . uh . . . start until about nine a.m. It will look almost full here around ten-fifteen."

Joanne remembered seeing a nearly total eclipse years before. Street lights came on and the birds chirped their evening songs. "But you keep looking at the sky. Expecting aliens to invade or something?"

Eric's reaction wasn't what she expected. "Why would you say that?"

"A joke," she said, holding up both hands as if defending herself from attack.

"Sorry I snapped," he said. "I've just got this headache."

"Probably from lack of sleep," Joanne suggested.

After that, she noticed him forcing himself to look anywhere but the sky. *Science nerds can be so weird.*

When they entered the diner, she nearly gagged on the strong stench. "What's that smell? Did they burn the coffee?" she said, covering her nose.

"Smells the same as always," Eric said.

She looked at him to be sure he wasn't joking. Not that she planned to drink the coffee anyway, but the smell took away any appetite she had.

Eric ordered the biggest breakfast the diner offered: French toast, three eggs, hash browns, a grilled blueberry muffin, bacon and sausage. Then he added a stack of pancakes, and in addition to his black coffee, a large orange juice and a hot chocolate with whipped cream.

"I know you like a big breakfast, honey, but don't you think you're overdoing it a bit? You might regret all those calories."

"Nope. From now on, I regret nothing," he said as he poured syrup over nearly the entire mess.

Joanne looked away. She'd ordered a dry English muffin with a side of peanut butter and a decaf ginger tea. She remembered the nurse saying that protein was supposed to help, but there was no way she could face an egg today.

His cell chirped again. Eric did the same thing he'd been doing all day: checked the text, frowned, then put the phone back in his pocket.

"What's with all the texts?"

"Oh, it's nothing. Just work."

He excused himself to go to the bathroom, leaving Joanne to ponder his odd behavior. He was hiding something. He didn't want to talk about the messages, but it wasn't the same kind of reluctance he usually had about discussing work. Something was different. If it weren't for that kiss this morning, and the flowers, and the . . .

Wait! she thought. *These could be the signs of a guilty conscience all right—but not about staying overnight at work. Exactly where was he all night?*

She had heard the tales before. Suddenly a husband gets romantic, but it's because he's been flirting—or worse—with another woman. There were plenty of women at work. Smart women—smarter than her, Joanne knew. Maybe she wasn't intelligent enough to keep him happy.

Could it be? Could he be attracted to someone else? Could he even be having an affair?

Then she thought about the baby. *Maybe if I'd told him already, he wouldn't have been interested in another woman. Maybe things wouldn't have gone this far—however far that is.*

Her mind raced. This was terrible. Would he ask for a divorce? Would their child grow up in a broken home? That was not the fairy tale they had dreamed of.

If she had to raise this child alone, how could she do it? She hadn't had a full-time job since being laid off at Sears. She didn't make enough money to support herself. And even with Eric's government job, they barely had enough for the little luxuries. She'd never be able to make it on child support alone. Where could they live? This was terrible!

Eric returned to the table, and Joanne felt tears fill her eyes.

"What's wrong?" Eric asked, signaling the server for a refill of his coffee.

"You tell me," Joanne said, sticking out her chin. She would be brave. She was strong. She had to be. She was going to be a mother.

Eric looked uncomfortable. "What have you heard?"

"Heard? Nothing. But I'm not a complete idiot, no matter what you might think. I can read the signs."

He glanced out the window. "What signs?"

"All of them," she said, giving him her best attempt at a hairy eyeball.

The goddamn cell chirped again.

"I'm sorry," he said after checking the text. "I have to make a call."

He took his phone and walked away from the table and right out the door. He wanted privacy. It must be *her*.

She decided to follow. He stood just outside with his back to the front door. Cracking the diner door open, she listened to Eric's side of the conversation.

"No, I don't think that's a good idea," he said. A long pause followed. "It might be hard for her to accept, but it's just too late."

Too late for what? To repair our marriage? She felt new tears sting her eyes.

Eric turned, and Joanne let the door close between them. She bolted back to their table in time to prevent the busboy from clearing their plates. Eric still had half of his breakfast to consume.

Her fears confirmed, Joanne rethought the romantic announcement of her pregnancy. *I won't tell him at all. That'll serve him right. I'll move to another state and he'll never meet his child. I won't let that creep anywhere near my baby. How could he do this to me?*

Then she thought about her baby growing up without a father. She knew that wasn't ideal either. *But to grow up with a cheating father—and maybe a floozy step-mother? No. Intolerable.*

It was a few minutes before Eric returned to the table. His breakfast looked soggy and congealed. It was all Joanne could do to keep from sweeping it off the table and into his lap.

"So, what was *that* all about?" she said, hoping her voice dripped with venom.

"Something at work."

That's all the explanation I get? Oh—I guess he's waiting for just the right moment to dump me like a sack of garbage. And to think that I was waiting for the right moment to give him the best news of his life. Well, you can forget that, buster.

"I don't think I want to go out today," Joanne said, folding her napkin. "I have things I need to do at home." *Like find a good lawyer.*

Eric looked up. His eyes betrayed disappointment. "Well, if you'd really rather. I guess we can see the eclipse from there, but it would be better without so many trees around."

"Well, that's what I want."

She refused to look at him, let alone speak to him, on the ride home.

It's still a couple of hours before the eclipse begins. I'm going to call Roger. He probably hasn't left for work yet," Eric said as they entered the house.

Joanne couldn't believe her ears. "Your brother, Roger?" *Couldn't you come up with a better excuse than that? You haven't spoken to your brother in six years, and now you expect me to believe you're going to call him for no reason?*

"Yeah. I just think it's time, you know?"

"Whatever."

Joanne went to their room and pulled out her own cell. Who did she know who would know a good divorce lawyer? Gloria, of course. She'd been divorced twice and was living comfortably on her former husbands' money. And, fortunately for Joanne, she was an early riser.

"Oh no, honey," Gloria said when she heard why Joanne called.

"No—you don't know a good lawyer?" Joanne asked.

"Oh, of course I do. I know more than one, but I'm just sorry that's something you need. I never would have guessed it of Eric. How long have you two been married?"

"Seven years."

"Oh—well, that's one of the dangerous years."

Gloria gave her three lawyers' names and their phone numbers. "They're the best in town. Make sure you meet with them all so Eric can't get any of them to represent him. Conflict of interest, you know. But make sure you hire the first name. She's the one I use."

"I would never have thought of that. Anything else I need to know?"

"It would be great if you could get proof of infidelity. I hired a PI, but sometimes you can find things on your own, like motel charges on the credit card—that kind of thing."

"Okay. Thanks, Gloria. It sounds like it's going to be expensive."

"Maybe, but I'm living proof that it's worth it in the long run."

After hanging up, Joanne knew where she had to start. She had to get a look at that cell phone and find out who the bimbo was.

Eric joined her in the bedroom looking ashen. "Well, that was tough," he said. "At first, Steph couldn't get Roger to come to the phone. Then when he did, he wouldn't talk. He just said, 'You called. Just tell me what you have to say.'"

"So you really called Roger?"

"Yeah. I said I was." He rubbed his temples. "Got any aspirin?"

"In the medicine cabinet. And what did you expect, calling out of the blue like that?" she snapped, annoyed that he had made her feel sorry for him.

Eric shook his head. "Yeah well, it's done." He looked at his phone and put it in his pocket.

How can I get a look at that phone? Joanne thought about it. There was only one thing that came to mind.

"I've changed my mind. Let's go to the lake."

Eric's face brightened. "Really? Great. I'll pack a cooler."

"Don't forget your bathing suit," Joanne called after him.

"Oh right," he said, returning to the bedroom and pulling it out of a drawer. "I'll be ready in ten minutes. I have special glasses for us to use." He gave her a serious look. "This is going to be fun."

Oh yeah. Tons of fun.

***

The trip took more than half an hour, but Eric didn't waste any time. Moments after arriving, he had stripped down to his swim trunks and t-shirt, locking his clothes in the car. As he spread a blanket on the sand of the nearly deserted beach, Joanne told him she was going to the bath house to change, but instead she went to the parking lot.

His phone was in his pants pocket. She turned it on and was glad, despite his penchant for secrets, that he didn't use the thumbprint recognition lock that came with the phone. She easily guessed his swipe pattern on the number pad—a lower-case "e" for Eric. She was in.

She scrolled through the texts. The most recent ones were from "Driscoll." She tried to remember if Eric had ever mentioned her. She opened the conversation.

Text from Driscoll at 5:46 am: "Procedure failure confirmed. Sorry."

That doesn't sound too sexy.

Text from Driscoll 6:14 am: "No other options available. Time now very short."

Options for what? Sounds kind of dire.

Text from Driscoll at 6:58 am: "Dr. Steinmetz agrees our assessment. Wants to discuss possible last-ditch approach."

Text from Driscoll at 7:10 am: "Please call me."

This was while we were at the diner. It must have been this Driscoll person that he called. What did he say again? Something about it being too late. Too late for what?

Then it hit her. These texts weren't from some girlfriend, nor were they about some illicit attraction. They were talking about something medical. Driscoll must be a nurse or a PA or something who works for this doctor Steinmetz. *Since when has Eric been going to a Doctor Steinmetz?*

She used the phone's browser to check on a doctor by that name in the area. She found several with a variety of specialties, but the only one that seemed to fit the texts was a neurosurgeon.

Oh no! Eric has a brain aneurysm. They tried some procedure, but it didn't work. He's going to die.

Just moments before she was imagining the satisfaction of murdering him, but now, discovering he was dying left her sobbing and gasping for breath.

It all made sense now. Wanting to spend a whole day with her. Calling his mother—and his estranged brother. Wanting to spend time at the lake while he could still enjoy it. The headache. Even eating like there was literally no tomorrow.

And what had she done but make it hard on him to spend one of his last days the way he wanted to.

Why hadn't he told her? They could have gone through this together. She could have helped him. He didn't have to keep her in the dark. But she would act as if she didn't know, since that was how he wanted it.

He didn't even know yet that he was going to be a father. Forget the romantic scene. She had to tell him now.

She locked the car and raced back to the beach, hoping to find Eric on the shore and not somewhere in the lake. He was standing near the water, staring at the sky through some strange dark glasses.

She came up behind him, focusing on where he was looking, straining to figure out what fascinated him so. It looked like the moon was up during the day—only brighter than usual. Almost like a second sun. *Must be some kind of Supermoon or something.* No wonder a science nerd would be interested.

She put her hand on his shoulder. "Darling, come with me. There's something I need to tell you."

Eric took off his glasses and gave her a quiz-zical look but followed her to a picnic table in the shade. He blinked several times while his eyes adjusted to the change in the light. They sat opposite each other, and Joanne took his hands in hers.

"I've been trying to find the perfect time to tell you this," she began. "I'm two months preg-nant. You're going to be a father."

Eric gasped. "You're . . . you're pregnant?" His face was wet with tears. "After all this time you're pregnant *now*?"

Joanne hadn't seen him cry since his father died before they were married. "I know. It's a miracle."

And for the first time, she realized that it was more than the fulfillment of their mutu-al dream. This child was a way for her to hold onto the husband she loved, even after he was gone. She would be sure that the baby learned everything about its father so that it never felt it didn't have a dad.

As soon as Eric gained control of his emo-tions, he lost it again. It took several tries for him to stop his tears. Joanne waited, wondering whether he would share his sad news with her.

"Do you know if it's a boy or a girl?" he asked.

"No. It's too early to know," she said. "But I hope it's a boy who will grow up to be like you."

Eric struggled to maintain his control. The sun on the beach had grown brighter, and the sand look electrified. Even in the shade sweat stung her eyes. Eric looked up at the sky, but Joanne held her gaze on him. He looked healthy—well a bit pale from not getting much sun this summer, but still, no one would guess he had an aneurysm.

"Tell me what you're thinking," Joanne prompted, hoping he'd let her in on his dark secret.

"That's classified," he said with a smirk.

"Does that really matter now?"

Eric looked at her and sighed. "Perhaps not," he admitted. "You seem to have an inkling anyway."

Joanne nodded. "Go on."

"Well my work at the Jet Propulsion Lab is in the Center for Near Earth Object Studies. In a nutshell, we look for things flying around in space in Earth's neighborhood."

Joanne had no idea where he was going with this.

"Most of these objects, comets, asteroids, and the like, are harmless to the Earth, but they can offer us information on the formation of the universe." Eric became more animated as he spoke.

Joanne smiled. *He really loves his work.*

"The gravitational pull of other bodies in space affect orbits of these Near Earth Objects, and if something happens to one of them that changes its gravitational pull, it affects the others as well. Am I going too fast?"

"No. I get it. But I wanted to know about your . . . headache."

"I'm getting to that." Eric said. "Our solar system is pretty stable. Our sun is too small to be at risk of ever going nova, and our planets are too far apart to affect each other's orbits."

"So . . . ?"

"But these 'NEOs' as we call them, we theorize that some don't just stay within our solar system. They travel to other parts of the universe where other forces can affect their trajectories in ways we can't predict. Okay so far?"

"Yes, but what does that have to do—"

"So, there are lots of comets and asteroids flying around. Some we know about and can predict. Others we can't. When that happens, if it looks like an Earth impact is imminent, we do what we can to avoid a collision, but our science isn't there yet. We can't change physics no matter how many late nights we spend trying to." He looked into Joanne's eyes as if asking, "Do you understand?"

Joanne was flummoxed. She had to take control of this conversation. "What does this have to do with you seeing a doctor?"

"What doctor?"

"Doctor Steinmetz. I saw the name on your phone in a message from somebody named Driscoll."

Eric rolled his eyes. "Larry Driscoll is a colleague. Doctor Steinmetz is in another division at JPL. We consult with her from time to time on these things."

"No, no. This Driscoll performed a procedure and told you there wasn't anything left to do. Then Doctor Steinmetz wanted to talk to you about another possible treatment. You don't have to hide it from me anymore. I saw the texts."

"Okay, but what you don't know . . . here, put these on." Eric handed her the glasses. "Now look." Eric pointed at the sky.

Joanne looked up. The moon had doubled in size and brightness. "What's happening to the moon? Is it falling out of the sky?"

"It's not the moon," Eric said. "It's bigger."

Joanne looked from Eric to the object, and back to Eric. "Is it going to hit us?"

Eric looked at his hands.

She stood, not wanting to believe what she now knew to be true. "Is it going to destroy us?" She so wanted to hear that everything was going to be okay, but Eric said nothing. She felt dizzy and sat down. "Why don't people know about this?"

"What's the point? Let people enjoy their day. Go to their eclipse parties. There's nothing they can do to get away from it. Nothing to be gained by sending the public into a panic." He swallowed hard. "Do you really want the last hours of humanity on Earth to be consumed with killing, looting, and suicides?"

"Or maybe prayer," Joanne said.

The heat from the approaching object intensified. It looked larger than the sun.

"It's coming fast, isn't it? We won't be here to see the eclipse." She felt nauseated and knew it wasn't morning sickness.

Eric shrugged. "It doesn't matter anymore."

"But the baby . . ." Joanne choked on the words and covered her belly with both hands.

"Will go with us," Eric said. "We'll all go together."

"It's not fair. Just when we were about to have a family, everything ends? It's not right."

"It doesn't matter anymore," he repeated.

"What will it be like?" she asked, her head throbbing.

"The heat will become more intense. We'll all pass out long before impact."

Joanne felt goosebumps despite the rising temperature. "Is this what it means to go into the light?"

Eric thought about his answer. "For us it is. It's what I came here to see."

Leaning on each other, they returned to the beach, staggering across the searing sand to their blanket. It was getting hotter by the second, and too bright to keep their eyes open even with the dark glasses.

They lay beside each other on the blanket, and she felt Eric kiss her. She reached for him, and they embraced as the fireball filled the sky.

The Hunt

The hunter crept across the deep-green carpet. His prey dawdled mere yards away, apparently unaware of his approach. He crouched down, eyes trained on the beast, watching for any sign of alarm. Nothing yet, but the hunter's nerves sharpened, alert to any risk of flight. He struggled to quell an involuntary twitch of his upper lip as he slunk forward, careful not to make a sound.

He thought about his circumstances. If he could, he would take a life today. And without remorse. Why was that old song running through his head? Was it from the movie *Aladdin* that the kids played incessantly when they were young? The line "gotta eat to live, gotta steal to eat. . . ." But in this case, he wasn't planning to steal. He would kill if he had the chance.

He wasn't very hungry, but he knew that if he did not take this opportunity it might be many days before he found such easy prey again. By then he could starve. No. He had to strike now and secure a meal while he could, to keep hunger at bay for another day.

Another day.

And what did he have to look forward to in the days to come? More of the same? Seeking food, clean water, and a safe place to rest. His demands were few, but they were crucial to his survival. He needed to keep his strength up to avoid becoming prey to a larger beast. As age slowed his reflexes, it was more important than ever.

His target froze. Had it become aware of his approach? Crouching lower, the hunter took aim. It was now or never. He had to make his move.

Flinging out his front paws, he pounced. The housefly sped off toward the ceiling and up the staircase. The hunter followed for a few steps, but decided instead to take a bath, turning his humiliation into the appearance of a choice. Besides, his human should be home soon.

There was, after all, more than one way to feed a cat.

A Late
Afternoon Visitor

My grandmother clears her throat with determination. I didn't notice her come in, but looking up from my book, I see her sitting in her favorite rocker across from me. She's wearing a hippie-style floral shirt, olive-green bell-bottoms, orange flip-flops, and a vintage Phillies baseball cap. I'm surprised I didn't hear her outfit enter the room.

"Whoa, Grams," I say, my heart flipping over. "It's so good to see you." I know I'm wearing the same broad smile her visits always evoke. "You surprised me."

"You were reading, as usual," she says, a mock rebuke in her voice. "No wonder you didn't hear me come in. You know, you'll ruin your eyes reading without a light on."

"My eyes are already ruined," I tell her, taking off my reading glasses and turning on the lamp to dispel the October dusk. "Besides, if I read too much it's your fault. You're the one who always read to me and took me to the library."

She clicks her tongue and gathers her lips in a tuft of wrinkles.

I smile, remembering summer days spent at Grams' and Granddad's house. She was the thinker; he was the doer. Granddad was always puttering around, fixing stuff, tending his garden, and keeping their old Victorian house in prime condition. Grams was the philosopher. We'd sit together on the porch swing, sipping homemade lemonade, and discussing the important minutiae of life. She'd tell me to be true to myself and not worry about what the other kids thought. She and I always had a special connection. We understood each other as well as any two people on Earth. Every kid should have such a childhood.

"So, what are you reading today?" she asks, nodding at my book.

"Persuasion," I say, pulling on my cardigan.

"Ah, Jane Austen."

"It's my favorite." I know my smile is a bit sheepish.

"I seem to remember that the first time you read it you didn't like it. You said Anne Elliot was mopey and moony and you didn't care if she lived happily ever after." We both laugh at the child I once was. We always laugh when we're together. "But the book seems to have—"

"—grown on me? Yes, it has." I know this pleases her. Persuasion is her favorite Austen, too. "I think reading Jane Austen with you is one of the reasons I decided on an English major in college."

"Good choice. I know some people think you should choose a major that will lead to a career, but I think you go to college to get an education, not a job. And what better major than English?"

"Well, it certainly isn't a vocational degree."

"Don't you worry. With your brains, you'll do fine."

I sigh, thinking about my "career" working at an indie bookstore for little more than minimum wage, supplemented by teaching a few English as a Second Language courses at the local community college.

"Speaking of Austen, have you ever noticed that all of her heroines get married at the end of the books?" Gram's eyes twinkle with mischief.

Okay—we're on that topic. "True," I say, "but we don't know whether they all lived—"

"—happily ever after?" She shakes a finger at me as she finishes my sentence. "I'm confident she wouldn't create those wonderful characters and not give them happy marriages in the chapters left unwritten," she says, cocking her head.

"Maybe," I say. "Jane Austen was once engaged, but she never married. Maybe that's why those books all stop at the engagement. Maybe she didn't know how to write about happily married people."

Grams shrugs, then locks her eyes on me. She is not to be deterred. "So, is there a special young man in your life these days?"

"Sadly, no." I'm not really sad about it; I'm just sorry to disappoint her.

"Well, you're not getting any younger, you know."

You have no idea, Grams. I reach up and pull my graying hair into a knot.

"While books can be good company," she continues, "there's no substitute for a life mate." She sits back and knits her fingers together across her tummy. "Look at Granddad and me."

I let out an involuntary sigh. "Not everyone is as lucky as you and Granddad," is all I can think of to reply. "Tell me, how is Granddad?" I say, trying to change the subject.

She looks confused for a moment. "He's happy." She looks upward past her wrinkled brow. "He sends his love," she says at last.

"Thanks for that." I smile, thinking of the black-and-white wedding photo that now sits on top of my dresser. Grams in a long white dress—Granddad, with a full head of hair, standing tall in his Navy uniform. They got married just as World War II began. My dad was on the way before Granddad shipped out. "Give him my love, too. I miss him."

Grams nods. "Then why don't you come to visit?" It isn't an accusation; she seems genuinely confused.

Her question pulls at my heart. "You two . . . moved so far away, Grams," I say. "But I think of you every day, and I'm always thrilled when you come back for a visit."

"Florida isn't the dark side of the moon, you know," she says, raising one eyebrow.

She's right. It isn't, but . . .

"Have you seen Lucy lately?" I say, hoping she's visited my little sister.

"Oh, that Lucy!" she says, slapping her knee. "She said the funniest thing the other day. What was it now? . . . Oh, I forget, but she's such a little card."

Yep—that's Lucy. If she's a card, she's the Queen of Diamonds. Gorgeous, funny, talented. She married a zillionaire high-tech geek who sold it all and "retired" at thirty-eight. They moved to Bimini with their two kids and priceless designer dogs. She's certainly living happily ever after. But I know she misses Grams as much as I do and would love a visit. For some reason, though, Grams never goes there. Maybe she just doesn't know how to get to Bimini.

Despite Lucy's good fortune, I know I'm the lucky one. By the time Lucy was old enough to spend time at Grams' and Granddad's house, they'd moved to a retirement community in Florida. She never got to help Granddad weed his garden or harvest the sunflower seeds he grew to feed the birds. She never got to spend days in the library or read with Grams on the porch swing.

"You've always been special to me," Grams says, winking. "And I love our little chats."

I sense she's getting ready to go. My eyes fill, and there's a lump in my throat. "And you've always been special to me." We grin at each other like a pair of carved pumpkins. I look at my grandmother's sparkling eyes and crazy clothes. To her, I'm still nineteen, still that college sophomore deciding to major in English, still with a lifetime of possibilities ahead of me.

"And all I want is for you to be happy, dear." Her voice cracks just the tiniest bit.

I consider my life. My marriage fell apart before the first anniversary, and my only other serious relationship ended in a lot of heartache instead of the life-long happiness she had with Granddad. But I remain true to myself, and at forty-seven and single, I have a great circle of friends. I'm using my English degree doing work I love. I live in a ground-floor apartment in their old Victorian house, tend Granddad's garden growing sunflowers to feed the birds, and sit on our porch swing to consider the minutiae of my life.

Then I look at Grams. She looks just as she did on that terrible day in 1985 when she and Granddad were driving along Highway 19 and were T-boned in an intersection by a truck driver blinded by the setting Florida sun.

As bad as that day was, I soon discovered that I didn't really lose them both. Grams still comes by every now and then—just to reassure me with her smile and remind me that I'm special to someone who is special to me.

"Don't worry about me, Grams," I say as I watch her fade from view. "I am happy . . . happy ever after."

We Gather Together

Rosy couldn't wait for her three kids to return home for the Thanksgiving weekend. She shopped, and cooked, and prepared their rooms with clean, cartoon-character sheets.

She'd done her job well. Now a lawyer, a schoolteacher, and a banker, her kids were all grown up. Pride filled her heart.

"That's *my* seat," said the banker as they gathered in the living room. The schoolteacher stuck out her tongue. The lawyer played video games with the volume too high for conversation. Dirty dishes littered every surface.

They'll go home soon, Rosy thought. *Not quite all grown up after all.*

Dora's Chocolate Cake

Every family has its food traditions, and in my family some of our favorites revolve around baking. We have Mom's traditional coffee cake—one we all love, but for some reason only make at Christmas. Then there's Grandpa's blueberry pie, made with fresh, wild blueberries he picked himself and made with Great-Aunt Ruby's flaky pie crust, which is our taste of summer. Uncle Dick's cheesecake is a must when entertaining visitors.

But, of all our baking traditions, one stands above the others: Dora's chocolate cake. It is our favorite birthday cake. No light, fluffy, many-layered cake for us. We opt for our rich, moist, brownie-like cake with velvety fudge frosting nearly every time one of us completes another circuit of the sun.

The original recipe came to our ancestor, Dora, from the mother of a friend over a century ago when Dora was still a young woman. Dora would make the cake for every occasion:

a picnic with friends, a potluck at church, a housewarming, and, of course, a birthday. She was famous for it.

Dora's original copy of the recipe was barely more than a list of ingredients. It goes back to the days when bakers knew the difference between a pinch and a dash. They knew flour was never "pre-sifted" and mixers were spun by hand. Most of us in the later generations have filled our recipe cards with the notes we less accomplished bakers need, but we all adhere to the recipe very carefully because we know the story about Dora's sister-in-law, Lilah.

Lilah and Dora weren't exactly close. On the day of Dora's wedding, Lilah dressed in black and moaned, "Oh, my poor brother. My poor, poor brother." Needless to say, the relationship between the two women was never warm. Heated, sometimes, but never warm.

Lilah was the baby of the family, and resented that her brother's attentions focused on his wife, and eventually their children, instead of on her. Even after Lilah married, she competed with Dora over silly things, such as who knit better, who kept a better home, and most of all, who was the better cook. On the last of these, Lilah felt she had the advantage.

Dora was a very good cook who always followed a recipe. Lilah, like her mother, was an instinctive cook. She could make nearly anything without requiring directions and would improvise even when she had a recipe to follow. She was never at a loss for what to make for dinner, because she could make a meal from whatever she had on hand. It was her strength, and she was extremely proud of it. Not surprisingly, she really resented the popularity of her sister-in-law's chocolate cake. She tried to devise a competing formula, but never found anything to compare with it. Finally, she asked Dora for the recipe.

Dora wrote out a recipe card for her, as she had done for dozens of friends over the years. The next day, Lilah made the cake, but she was disappointed with the results.

"Dora, you didn't give me the right recipe," Lilah accused her over the phone. "It didn't come out the same."

"No, Lilah," Dora told her. "I copied the recipe I use exactly."

"No you didn't. You left something out. You just don't want anyone else to make your precious cake."

Dora shook her head. "Now, Lilah, I wouldn't do that. I've given that recipe out lots of times before and no one else has had any problem with it."

"Are you saying I'm not a good enough baker to make your silly cake?" Lilah's voice was shrill.

"Not at all," Dora said after returning the phone to her ear, "but you need to follow the recipe precisely. You cannot improvise, or make any substitutions, or it won't come out the same."

"I am still *sure* you left something out. Just give me the recipe again. Then we'll see."

"Okay, here it is," Dora said, cradling the phone on her shoulder and getting out the recipe card. "But remember to follow it exactly."

"I *will*."

Dora began, "The first ingredient is four ounces of unsweetened baking chocolate . . ."

"Okay . . ." Lilah said. "Um, how much is that in cocoa?"

***

After many years of being told her chocolate cake was the best, Dora developed a certain proprietary pride in it. So, many years later, when women at her office compared notes on their favorite recipes, she was certain that her cake would stand up against the challenge of another who claimed she had the best of all possible chocolate cake recipes.

"I hate to tell you, Dora," said Evelyn, "I am sure yours is good, but mine is indisputably the best. I had it once at the Waldorf-Astoria Hotel when I was on a trip to New York City. I was so taken with it, that when I returned home, I wrote to them and asked for the recipe. I didn't know whether or not they would share it, but I figured that if they didn't, all I'd lost was the three-cent stamp for the letter."

The women all nodded. It seemed worth a try.

"So, imagine my surprise when, a little while later, an envelope arrived with a return address from the Waldorf-Astoria. Inside was not only the recipe for their chocolate cake, but a bill for one-hundred dollars."

A general gasp ensued, for in those days one-hundred dollars was a small fortune.

"What did you do?" the coworkers wanted to know.

"I didn't really think I had any choice," she said, "so I paid the bill. But I have made a point of sharing that recipe with everyone who asks for it since then. I want to get my money's worth out of it."

It certainly seemed as though Dora's cake might have met its match. Still, the proof of the pudding—or in this case the cake—is in the tasting, so the two women agreed to go home, bake their respective cakes, and bring them into the office for their colleagues to decide which was better. And each one would bring her recipe to share with their friends.

No one was out sick on the day of the taste-off.

Dora's cake sat on her desk, and Evelyn's on hers. They looked the same. They smelled enticing. It was difficult, but the women waited until lunch before cutting into either cake and serving them to their coworkers. And, of course, Evelyn and Dora had to taste each other's.

Dora took a bite of Evelyn's, and let it sit on her tongue. Then, she moved it around her mouth, trying to savor every last nuance of its texture and flavor. It was, Dora had to admit, a wonderful cake. She looked over at Evelyn, who was testing Dora's cake with the same attention to detail. They put their forks down and looked at each other. Neither wanted to be the first to speak. While their colleagues raved about both cakes, the two bakers knew which one was superior.

"Your cake is better," they each said at the same time. Then, realizing what had happened, they broke into a laugh. The tension relieved, they freely agreed that while the cakes were very similar, they each enjoyed the one baked by the other woman better.

"Well, I can't tell them apart," said a coworker. "They are both wonderful. I couldn't pick between them."

Neither Evelyn nor Dora thought so, however. They got out their recipe cards to see where the minor differences in ingredients or proportions were. They swapped cards, so each could review the other's. As they read, their expressions changed from curiosity, to confusion, to amusement. The two recipes were identical.

"I guess it's true," Dora said, "food tastes better when someone else does the cooking."

Everyone in the building got a recipe card that day. And since then, in our family, it has been known as Dora's "Hundred-Dollar Cake."

The Dream

"I dreamt about Edward last night," Father said at breakfast. My little brother Joey and I were much more interested in the fact that it was Christmas Eve than in any old dream, but Mama reacted sharply.

"Edward? Why ever did you dream of him?" she asked. "He's been gone now, well, I suppose it's been about five years."

"Five exactly," Father said. "It was such a real dream. He was out in our old rowboat in the middle of the lake, and when he saw me, he raised his arm and beckoned for me to join him," Father said with an uncomfortable laugh. Then he waved his arm to imitate what he saw in his dream, a tear appearing in the corner of his eye. "It's left me quite melancholy for him, I'm afraid."

"Why?" I said. "What happened to him?"

Father looked at me as if he hadn't noticed I was there. Then he glanced at Mama who shook her head. I knew that meant that she didn't want him to tell me whatever it was. But Father's eyes told me he thought I was old enough to know.

"You were just a sapling, little one," he said. "Not much more than a baby then."

"I'm not a baby now," I said, straightening up to my full height. Father looked at Joey, who was running his fork along the table and making rumbling sounds with his mouth, pretending his fork was a truck.

Father sighed. "I guess you're old enough to know." He folded his napkin and put his face close to mine.

"Just after you were born, your Uncle Edward moved to California."

I had heard of California. I had some cousins there that I never expected to meet because it was over a thousand miles from our home in Kansas.

"Before that, we used to go fishing together a lot," Father continued. "We would sit in the boat with our lines in the water, and your uncle would tell me the biggest tall tales you ever did hear. I used to say the only reason we ever caught any fish was because all them big ones swam up to our boat, so they could hear what Edward would say next." Father laughed, like he was halfway back in that old boat with Uncle Edward, hearing him tell a tall tale.

"Then what happened?" I said, not wanting Father to forget he was telling a story of his own.

"Well, then, we got a telegram on Christmas Day, five years ago. It said that Edward was getting ready to go to church on Christmas Eve. He was wearing his best clothes, and had just finished slicking down his hair, when he dropped his comb on the floor. Next thing they knew . . ." Father snapped his fingers close to my nose and I blinked. "He keeled over dead. Just like that." He shook his head. "I just wish I'd known our last fishing trip was to be our last one ever." I could hear regret in his voice, and it made me feel sad.

"That's enough of that," Mama said. It's Christmas Eve, and I need these children to help with the baking instead of lollygagging with you all day, old man. She shooed Father out of the kitchen, and, as soon as she finished washing the dishes and I dried them all, we got to work on our cookies.

We spent the whole day with Mama. I don't remember what Father did. He might have gone to work. All I remember is that by the time Mama was making supper, he came into the kitchen. He still looked sad, and I wanted to cheer him up.

"Look at all the sugar cookies we made," I said, waving my arm at the piles of cookies cooling on brown paper on the table. It was my job to package them up so we could take them to church to hand out to our friends and neighbors. "We've got enough for the whole world."

Father barely looked at the pile. I asked Mama if he could have a one. Joey had already taken a piece of a broken cookie and was licking the crumbs off his fingers.

"No cookies for me," Father said. I could tell he was still thinking about Uncle Edward. I didn't know how to make him feel better.

I wrapped bundles of cookies, and then set the table, still trying to figure out how to make Father feel better. It was Christmas Eve. Shouldn't he be happy?

Father was quiet at dinner, but Joey was a chatterbox. He talked about Santa Claus and whether he would get the toy truck he asked for. He didn't understand about Father feeling sad.

After supper and washing up, Mama sent us to our rooms to get gussied up for church. Joey could pretty well dress himself, but sometimes it was hard to get him to wear the stuff Mama had put out for him. I got my dress on all right, but I couldn't do up the buttons on the back, so I went into Mama and Father's room for help.

"Come here, child," Mama said. "Now pull your hair up while I button those buttons."

I turned my back to Mama and pulled up my hair. It smelled like cookies. I looked over at Father who winked at me as he buttoned his own shirt. I laughed. Maybe he was starting to feel better. "Oh look," he said, pointing to the window. "It's snowing."

I looked out and saw big, fluffy flakes drifting by the street lamp.

"I hope it doesn't pile up too fast," Mama said. "It might be hard to drive home after church."

"I wouldn't worry," Father said, pulling up his bright red suspenders. Then he picked up his comb to neaten up his hair. He was halfway through, when he turned back to me with a look of surprise on his face. Then he dropped his comb and fell to the floor. He didn't move.

At first, I laughed. I thought he was making a joke, and I was glad he was in a better mood. But then Mama rushed over to him and called out his name. She felt his neck. Then she let out a wail I'll never forget.

Christmas was never the same after that. Mama, Joey, and I stopped going to church. "I'm not fit company on Christmas Eve," Mama said, and we never questioned it. We didn't feel like celebrating, either. Even Joey, who only had a few patchy memories about Father, knew better than to talk about Santa Claus or presents.

Years passed, and we grew up. I got married and moved to Nebraska. Joey became some kind of scientist and got a job in Oklahoma. Mama lived alone in our old house, and we'd come to visit with our children a couple of times a year. Then, one day in early December, she joined Father.

We all gathered for her funeral, and I stayed on at the old house, going through stuff and settling Mama's affairs. Joey took time off from work to help.

"Stay for Christmas," I said to him. "It will take me at least that long to get everything settled. Besides, since I got married, I've found joy in Christmas again. Hugh and the kids are coming, and I'd like to share it all with you."

Joey looked doubtful. "I can't stay that long," he said. "But maybe I can return."

I held him to his word, and, since Christmas was on a Monday, I invited him to come on Saturday and bake with me on Christmas Eve as we did all those years ago.

We sat across from each other, in the mid-afternoon of Christmas Eve, packing up homemade cookies for him to take with him. Hugh and the kids had gone off to a matinée at the old theater in town. I couldn't shake a certain sadness, knowing it was our last time together in Mama's house. Joey seemed sad, too.

"There is something about being back in this house," Joey said, biting a broken sugar cookie. "I even dreamt about Father last night."

I stopped sorting the cookies and looked up at him. "Wow. It's been so long. What did you dream?" I asked.

"It was the oddest thing," he said, licking the last crumbs from his fingers. "I don't remember ever going fishing with him, but I saw him out in a boat with some fishing rods, and he was waving for me to join him. It was so real."

"That *is* strange," I said, hoping my face wasn't as white as it felt. Was it poor insulation that caused a sudden chill in the old farmhouse kitchen?

For the rest of the day, I couldn't shake the sense of foreboding. I worried that something would happen to Joey if he stayed in the house that night. I told myself it was irrational, but I'd seen it happen before.

"You don't have to stay tonight," I said. "You probably want to get home for Christmas."

"That's okay. I said I'd stay," he said. "I don't want you to be left alone with all the work to do."

"I can handle it," I said. Joey was a scientist. I couldn't tell him the real reason I wanted him to go. He would just laugh.

"Besides, it's started snowing," he said, drawing back the curtain. "The traffic will be terrible."

I looked outside. Sure enough, fat flakes drifted by and settled in the brown grass.

"Anyhow," he said, scratching his head, "I'd rather be here with you for one last Christmas together."

"That's the problem," I blurted out. He gave me a quizzical look, but I felt compelled to go on. "It *will* be our last Christmas if you stay."

"What do you mean?"

I broke down as I told him the story about Father's Christmas Eve dream. "And you had that dream, too. If you stay . . ."

His look said, "You're nuts," but his words were more charitable. "C'mon, Sis. There's nothing to worry about. It's just a coincidence." He sounded so certain. "I must have heard that story somewhere along the line, so being back in the house just brought it back to me. The subconscious is capable of all kinds of tricks."

"I hope you're right," I said. "I guess it does sound a little silly, but it's just such an odd thing to dream—especially here—on Christmas Eve."

I turned and watched him as he pulled out his comb and tidied his hair. Then he looked at me with a puzzled expression . . . and dropped his comb.

You Better Watch Out!

"Great party, Joy," Wendell Owens said, taking a snowball cookie from the tray. "It just wouldn't be the Christmas season without your open house."

"Thanks, Wendell." Joy smiled at her guest. "For a while there, I wasn't sure I'd be able to put an open house together this year. I've been so busy at work."

"That would have been our loss," Wendell said. "Where would we all go after lighting the town Christmas tree?" Wendell was a jovial man, who, when suited up in red fur and supplied with a white beard, made a very convincing Santa Claus for the town tree lighting every first Friday of December. As a long-time resident, and publisher and editor of the New England village's weekly newspaper, he knew every child in town by name. When he handed out gifts at the town celebration, he always had a comment or two that made each child wonder how Santa really knew whether they had been bad or good that year.

"Well, I'm glad to help keep the town's disreputable characters off the streets." Joy laughed as she looked around at the members of the Board of Selectmen, the minister from the Congregational Church, the town's only doctor, and several of Joy's colleagues from her law practice who filled her living room. The church organist regaled the group with variations of songs of the season on Joy's upright piano.

The doorbell rang, barely audible over the laughter and music. Joy shook her head. "Don't they know it's an open house?" she said and handed her tray to her teenage daughter, Holly. "Take care of this for me, will you, sweetie?"

By the time Joy reached the front door, her husband, Nick, was already opening it. She could see the blue and black of the police officer's uniform and the reflection of his leather holster in the porch light.

"What's happened?" she asked, before Nick or the officer could speak.

"Accident," Officer Dan Davis said. "Dr. Barnes here?"

"Is someone hurt?"

"I got a call. Jimmy Kerrigan fell off his roof a few blocks down. He's in a bad way. His sister called for an ambulance. Figured since I was nearby I'd get Dr. Barnes if he's here."

"I'll get him," Joy said, turning toward her guests. She had no trouble picking out Dr.

Barnes. He was tall and thin, about forty, with a pock-marked face that looked like it never held a smile. He had just moved to town from Springfield to open a small practice and to take a job as a part-time medical examiner. People were glad to finally have a doctor in the community, but his permanently dour expression held friendly overtures at bay.

Joy approached him, but had to call his name before he noticed her. "Dr. Barnes, there's a police officer at the door."

The doctor flinched. "Why tell me?"

"They need you immediately. There's been an accident."

"Dead people aren't usually in much of a hurry," Dr. Barnes said with a scowl, "so this one must still be alive."

"Yes, and in need of medical attention. Please hurry." Joy took Barnes by the arm and led him to the door. "Do you have your medical bag?"

"In my car," Barnes said as he grabbed the coat Nick handed to him and left with the officer.

"Oh dear," Joy said to Nick as he closed the door. "I hope everything is all right. I feel like going over to see if there's anything I can do to help."

"You can't help the doctor, Joy. And you don't want to appear to be an ambulance chaser," Nick said with a wink.

Joy grimaced. "I guess you're right."

"Thanks for a wonderful time," Wendell said as he rushed past Joy and Nick, putting his coat on as he went. The life of a newspaperman was always subject to interruption.

"Now *he's* an ambulance chaser." Joy and Nick laughed after closing the door.

***

Once the party was over and the dishes done, Joy's thoughts turned to Jimmy Kerrigan. He was a life-long resident of the small town, and had run a local auto repair shop for several decades before selling it and retiring. Since then, he kept busy as a handyman. Joy guessed he must be in his late seventies. He and his sister, Margaret, lived in the modest house where they grew up.

Like his sister, Jimmy had never married. He was one of those local institutions whom everyone recognized and thought well of, but who never seemed to be part of any of the goings-on in town. An independent New Englander. Joy hoped his independent spirit would help him recover from his fall.

It was after one in the morning, and Joy couldn't sleep. Nick snored in the bed next to her, but she got up and walked into the hallway. She crept past Holly's room, across the hall to the spare bedroom that they used as a library, to look for a book to help her get to sleep. Once there, she decided to call the police department non-emergency number to see if she could get an update on Jimmy Kerrigan's condition.

"Well, you didn't hear it from me," the dispatcher told Joy, "but I hear he has some broken bones and he's in a coma."

"Do they know why he was on the roof?" Joy asked.

"His sister said he was trying to fix a skylight before that snow moves in tonight."

"In the dark? That doesn't seem like a very good idea, does it?"

"Turned out not to be." New England understatement.

***

By morning, the ground was covered with eight inches of new snow. Shortly after dawn, Nick was outside clearing their driveway and the sidewalk in front of their century-old house. Joy started the coffee maker and prepared milk and eggs so she could make French toast as soon as he came inside. She didn't expect to see Holly up for a while at least.

Joy settled down with the morning's Springfield *Republican*. There was a story about a man from Longmeadow who went to court to keep from having to tear down his stone wall, one about a Connecticut teen who robbed an old woman and was tracked all the way to Amherst, and a report on Christmas illustrations at the Norman Rockwell museum in Stockbridge. Nothing, of course, about Jimmy Kerrigan. She knew that Wendell Owens would cover the story in the *Town Monitor*, but it wasn't due out for another five days.

She thought about calling the police station again to find out what was going on. Instead, she started heating the griddle, and set the kettle to boil for a cup of tea. Before the teakettle whistled, Nick came onto the covered porch by the kitchen door, stomping snow off his boots. Joy poured a cup of coffee, and handed it to him as soon as he had his coat off.

"Thanks, hon." Nick smiled, removing his fogged-over sunglasses. "It's a nice packing snow out there." Nick's cheeks were bright red, and Joy could see a sparkle in his hazel eyes. It wasn't the first snow of the season, but so far it was the biggest. It seemed to have put Nick in the holiday mood.

"Maybe I can get Holly to build a snowman with me after she gets up." Nick's grin showed off his dimples. They always made Joy smile.

"I have two kids," Joy said, ruffling Nick's hair.

After breakfast was cleared away, something about the sun reflecting on the new snow drew Joy outside. "I think I'll take a walk, Nick," she said.

"Sure thing. Hey, if you're in town, could you pick up some bread? It looks like the French toast nearly wiped us out."

"Sure." Joy bundled up for the six-block walk. While some of the sidewalks were not yet cleared, the roads were cleaned down to wet pavement. An occasional car spit slush up along the curb, but Joy was quick enough to avoid being splashed. Turning a corner, she saw the proud blue spruce that always served as the town Christmas tree, glistening with new-fallen snow. Joy thought about the legend of Martin Luther seeing a snow-covered evergreen during an evening walk in the woods. It glowed in the moonlight, and left the religious reformer so awestruck that he brought a tree home and lit it with candles to share it with his family. Joy could understand his wonder when nature decorated itself so well.

She ducked into the local grocer's and picked up a loaf of bread. Walking along the town green, Joy smiled at the children shouting at each other from behind snow forts. Then she glanced into the windows of the various merchants, each with a new holiday display. When she came to the office of the *Town Monitor*, she peered in the front window, hoping to see Wendell inside. The office was dark.

"Casing the joint?" Joy jumped at the voice behind her. Turning, she saw Wendell carrying a box of doughnuts and a tall paper cup of coffee.

"Wendell! No—I was just wondering if you were inside."

"Nope, but if you'll wait a second, I will be." He pushed open the unlocked door. Joy followed.

The office smelled of stale coffee, dust, and old paper. He put the box of doughnuts down, and lifted the lid to offer one to Joy. She surveyed the array, all frosted and decorated with holiday sprinkles.

"Um, not for me. Thanks anyway."

"So," Wendell said, taking a bite of a chocolate frosted, "what brings you to my office?"

"I was just wondering what happened last night with Jimmy Kerrigan."

"Oh. Tough old buzzard, Jimmy. We got there before the ambulance. Dr. Barnes looked at him, and then the EMTs arrived and took him off to county hospital. I got some pictures for this week's paper."

Wendell pulled a digital camera out of a desk drawer and turned it on. "Here's where last night's pictures start."

Joy looked at the camera's display and saw a photo of Jimmy Kerrigan, lying on the ground, his face contorted in pain.

"He was conscious when you got there?" Joy asked.

"Yeah. He was mumbling something, but I couldn't make it out. Poor old guy."

Joy pushed a button, and the picture dissolved, revealing another. "What is Dr. Barnes doing?" Joy showed the newspaperman a photo of Dr. Barnes, with his head turned to the side, hovering over the injured man's face.

"Don't know. Listening for a heartbeat?"

Joy shook her head. "That's not his chest. Maybe trying to see if he's breathing?"

"That doesn't make sense. He was conscious."

"True. What did Dr. Barnes do for him?" Joy asked, handing the camera back to Wendell.

"Nothing much. The EMTs were there a moment after we got to the scene. They took over, and Barnes didn't even go in the ambulance. I guess the cops didn't need him after all. It worked out for me, though. I don't know how long it would have been before I heard about this if they hadn't come by your house to collect Dr. Barnes. And I wouldn't have gotten these pictures."

"What do you hear from the hospital?"

"Nothing. The hospital won't answer questions from the press due to patient privacy laws, and his sister isn't answering the phone. You know these old New Englanders. Their business is their business—not yours."

"Well, it's Saturday. Here's hoping that by Thursday, you have some good news to report in the paper."

"It'll have to come by Tuesday at four. That's when I have to send the paper to press."

"I hope he'll come around by then."

Something about the accident had put a damper on Joy's holiday spirit that even the splendor of the town Christmas tree could not dispel. Perhaps it was the way it had interrupted her holiday open house; maybe it was just because Jimmy Kerrigan was such a town institution. She shook her head as she walked home, the loaf of bread swinging at her side.

When she got home, she smiled at a small snowman standing in the yard. Inside, she found Nick in the library grading papers. He taught history at the county community college, and as the end of the semester approached, the term papers flowed in.

"I don't know why you assign so much work for your students," Joy teased him. "If you didn't assign it, you wouldn't have to grade it."

"And they would know no more at the end of the class than they did at the beginning." Nick grimaced and removed his reading glasses. "Although, from the look of these papers, I'm not sure how much they've learned."

"Poor baby," Joy cooed, rubbing Nick's shoulders. "That's a cute snowman outside. Where's Holly?"

"She went over to Bethany's house to work on some project for school."

"Great. How about I make us some lunch?"

***

After lunch, Nick took his coffee and returned to the library and his grading. Joy settled down at the dining room table with her address book and a couple of boxes of Christmas cards. It was the first weekend of December, but Joy knew that getting their cards out was a long process. She always tried to write a personal note in each one, and she had a feeling that would be hard for her to do this year. To help put her in the Christmas spirit, she put on some Christmas music, lit a fire in the living room fireplace, and made herself a cup of holiday-blend tea. Before long, she was humming along with "I'll Be Home for Christmas," and admiring her growing stack of completed cards.

That close to the winter solstice, the sun set early. By five o'clock it was fully dark outside, and Holly still had not returned from her friend's house. Joy texted her daughter's cell with a message that dinner would be at six. Then, she went to work preparing the meal.

With water running and pans rattling, Joy didn't notice any noises coming from outside. She flipped on the backyard light and smiled through the kitchen window at the bird tracks in the snow under the bird feeder. Nick kept it filled all winter long.

Just then, a load of snow fell from the roof, dropping past the window. Joy was surprised that it was warm enough after dark to melt the snow. Maybe they needed more attic insulation.

A pot of spaghetti sauce simmered on the stove as Joy prepared cutlets for chicken par-mesan. The windows steamed up as she boiled pasta. Cooking usually put Joy in a good mood, but the image of poor Jimmy Kerrigan, lying injured on the ground with Dr. Barnes hovering over him, was something she couldn't shake.

Just as she was about to drain the pasta, she sensed a presence behind her. She dropped the pot into the sink, and whirled around to find Nick leaning in for a hug.

"You scared me half to death."

"What? I was just coming in to see if I could help with dinner."

"I could have scalded us both. Never sneak up on a woman cooking pasta."

"I'll make a note of that. So, do you want me to make the salad?"

"Sure. I'll try to salvage the spaghetti. Is Holly home yet?"

"Haven't seen her; I've been upstairs grading."

"What could be taking her so long? Perhaps we should call Bethany's house and see if she has left yet."

Eeeeeeeeeek!

At the sound of a scream outside, Joy and Nick raced to the front door. Nick pulled it open to reveal Holly standing halfway up the front walk, clearly panicked, but apparently uninjured.

"What happened? Are you okay?" Nick yelled as he ran to his daughter.

"*Ohmigod,* Dad, are *you* okay? I thought I just saw you fall off of our roof!"

Joy followed Holly's frightened gaze. Outlined in the snow was the figure of a man, dressed in red fur with white trim, lying face down.

"Nick, call 9-1-1," Joy said, dashing over to the prone figure. "Wendell? Wendell! Are you all right? We're calling an ambulance. You're going to be fine." She touched the man's neck and felt for a pulse. She could not find any. She lifted the man's shoulder and tried to turn him onto his back so that she could start CPR.

"Uh, Mom, that's not Mr. Owens," Holly said, coming up behind her.

"What?" Joy asked, looking for the first time at the man's face. "Who is it?"

"I guess it's Santa."

***

Once the EMTs arrived, Joy took Holly inside to warm her up, and make sure she was no worse off for the shock she had received. Next, she called Wendell. She knew it was not he who had fallen on her lawn, but she needed to hear his voice to be reassured that he was all right.

"*Town Monitor*." Wendell answered the phone on the first ring.

"Wendell. It's Joy. There's been another accident, only this time it was at our house."

"Your house? Is anyone hurt? What happened?"

Joy took the phone to the window and watched as the police taped off the scene and the crime scene unit arrived. "We're okay, but someone has . . ." she had trouble saying the word. "I think someone has died."

"I'll be right over."

***

The next morning, the doorbell rang as Joy, Nick, and Holly were getting ready for church. Nick opened the door to Officer Dan Davis.

"Dan. Come in. Don't you even get Sundays off?"

"Not when there's been an unexplained death in town. And right after Jimmy Kerrigan's accident, too." He shook his head. "Why do people think it's a good idea to be up on a roof in the middle of winter?"

"Do you have any information on who that guy was, or why he was here?" Joy asked, joining the men in the living room.

"Yeah. I thought you folks would like to know. He didn't have any ID on him, but we ran his prints. He has a lot of aliases, but the name he uses most is Harry Watts. Does that ring a bell with either of you?"

Nick and Joy looked at each other, and shook their heads.

"He's a second-story man with a long rap sheet. I guess he decided to bring his business to town. Too bad he picked the night after a big snowstorm. You can see on your roof how he slid on the snow. Half of your roof is wiped bare." Joy remembered seeing snow fall past the kitchen window.

"A burglar? Here?" Nick said. "We haven't had any real crime in town as long as I have lived here. That's one of the reasons we like it. It's far enough away from the city to avoid their problems."

"Well, this guy's last known address was in Springfield. But city folk have cars, too. No one is safe these days. I wish I could convince more people to lock their doors."

"He came an awfully long way to die." Joy shuddered. "Do you have any idea why he was dressed as Santa Claus?"

"No real theories on that. And we can't ask him."

Nick shook his head. "Is there anything else we can help you with, Dan?"

"Nope. I think I got everything I needed last night. Let me know, though, if you think of anything, or remember ever running into this guy Watts. There will be an autopsy, of course, but I think we'll find that he died of . . . overconfidence."

***

Joy usually found that being at work pushed personal problems to the back of her mind, but the next day, she found it hard to concentrate. It's not every day that a man dies in your yard. She couldn't get the image of him lying in the snow out of her mind. What was he doing there? Why did he come all the way from Springfield to burglarize their house? And why was he dressed as Santa?

On her lunch break, she went over to the newspaper office, to see if Wendell had any more information on either of the two falls.

"From what I've been able to gather, there's no change in Jimmy's condition. The doctors don't know if he'll ever wake up," Wendell told Joy.

"How's his sister holding up?" Joy asked.

"Tough old bird. She's okay, and even if she weren't she wouldn't let anybody know it."

"What a terrible Christmas season this is. Do you know any more about this Harry Watts character?"

"My sources in Springfield confirm that he was in and out of jail most of his life. His last stint was for robbing the houses of the recently deceased while their families were burying them."

"I've heard of that happening. How awful to add such an injury to people who are already burdened with sorrow."

"I don't think that mattered much to him."

"But that really doesn't explain what happened here. Why would he come all the way from Springfield? And why would he dress as Santa?"

"No idea." Wendell shrugged. "I thought that was *my* thing," he added with a chuckle.

"And Nick and I were home. Is it likely he would change his M.O. so dramatically without a reason?"

"Maybe his reason was that he got caught with the old one."

Joy considered this, but it didn't seem to be a sufficient explanation. "No. It has to be something more. Something had to bring him here.

And I can assure you it was not our collection of paperback books and refrigerator art. Maybe he has a connection with someone in town. Do you know anyone with connections in Springfield?"

"Well, let's see. Most of the businesses in town probably have contacts there. It's a decent-sized city, after all. Some wholesalers there. I think the bank's regional corporate office is there. Not sure what else."

"I don't think that's it. It has to be more . . . I don't know. More personal, I guess."

"Oh, you mean like family in Springfield? Sure. Some folks probably have relatives there, or went to school there, or something like that. Hey, I think the Carlton's kid goes to college in Springfield."

Something had been nagging at the back of Joy's brain, but she couldn't bring it into focus. Then, she remembered. "I've got it. Dr. Barnes is from Springfield."

"True. But a lot of people are from Springfield, Joy. That doesn't mean anything. Just because he's an unpleasant SOB doesn't mean he's in cahoots with a burglar."

"But don't you see how it fits? Dr. Barnes is a medical examiner. Medical examiners know about who has died. He and Watts could have been working together all this time. So when Barnes moved, Watts came, too."

"But no one died at your house, Joy. In fact, no one has died in town all month, except for Watts. This would be a lousy place for him to take up his old habits."

Joy could not come up with a response. She really felt that she was onto something, but the pieces didn't fit. Or perhaps some of the pieces were still missing.

When she got home, she tried her theory on Nick. "Maybe," she said, "he was casing our house during the party, and that's why Watts came here."

"If he were casing our house, it wouldn't take him long to figure out we don't have much of any value," Nick said. "Don't let your imagination run away with you, Joy. Sometimes it's better to just let it go and be glad that Watts didn't harm anyone other than himself."

It always annoyed Joy when Nick accused her of having an over-active imagination, but she had to admit he had a point.

***

On Wednesday morning, Joy heard the good news. Wendell called her office to tell her that Jimmy Kerrigan had regained consciousness. He was still groggy, and did not remember the fall, but the prognosis was good. The news lifted Joy's spirits.

As expected, Thursday's *Town Monitor* had both falls on the front page. "Nightmares on Elm Street" read the somewhat hyperbolic banner headline. Joy was glad that at least one nightmare appeared to be nearing its end. Wendell had devoted the entire top of the paper to the two accidents and had included photos of each of the victims. Taking up three columns on the left-hand side of the paper was a subhead reading "Local injured on West Elm." Below it was an account of Jimmy Kerrigan's fall.

Wendell included comments from neighbors who were not surprised Jimmy tried to do the repairs himself. "He never met a job he didn't think he could handle," one friend was quoted as saying. "His work is always first rate," said another. A former customer of his garage said he was honest. There was even a quotation from someone who had known him since high school that mentioned his impish sense of humor. Reading it, Joy wished she had known him better.

Jimmy's photo, located next to the subhead, looked like it was taken about thirty years ago. *Wendell probably got it from his sister,* thought Joy. Of more interest to her, however, was the right-hand side of the page where two columns in a shaded box held a subhead reading "Suspect dies in fall on East Elm." The picture, located near the fold, seemed to be an old mug shot of Harry Watts. She looked at the photo, trying to see if she could discern anything familiar, but had no success. She scanned the article, mostly drawn, it appeared, from the archives of the Springfield *Republican*, with information on his last crime from Officer Dan Davis. Joy had not thought until that moment how nice it was that Wendell had not sought a comment from her, or worse from Holly, about the incident. Nothing in the article, though, gave her a clue as to why the man had chosen their home to burglarize.

Wendell had made good use of his photos, but readers had to open to page three to see them. The photo spread included several of Jimmy Kerrigan, lying on the ground, on a stretcher, and being loaded into an ambulance. The ones of Watts were less graphic, perhaps out of respect for the dead, or for the readers. They included one of the ambulance, a photo of Officer Davis giving an interview, and one of Watts' home in Springfield. While it seemed to Joy that the articles were complete and well-written, they yielded little new information. Joy sighed. What more could she expect?

Looking through the rest of the news, Joy saw that the high school holiday pageant would be performed Friday night, the choral society concert was set for Saturday, and the children's Christmas parade would be held downtown on Sunday afternoon at two. The last of these events usually brought out most of the town, and was followed by vigorous holiday shopping at the local merchants. For most of a week the dark cloud of the two accidents had hung over her community. Perhaps now their holiday celebrations could proceed unfettered.

***

The weather on Sunday was perfect for the children's parade. While Holly declared herself to be too old to participate in such things, Nick and Joy convinced her to come and watch, with the promise of an ice cream soda at the drug store afterward. As usual, most of the town was in attendance. Wendell was there with his camera taking photos of the crowd, awaiting the first group of marchers to come around from the parking lot behind the town hall and begin the route around the green.

Joy looked at the crowd, and noticed most of her guests from the open house were there. The Selectmen huddled together, and several of her coworkers stood with cameras at the ready to take pictures of their children. Even Jimmy Kerrigan's sister was there, surrounded by other women, all wearing red hats. Joy searched the sea of faces. Where was Dr. Barnes? She could not silence her lingering suspicions about the man. Then she looked again at Margaret Kerrigan.

"I've got it!" Joy said, grabbing Nick's arm. "I know what happened."

"Huh?" he said, looking toward the town hall.

"Where's Dan Davis? I need him." She found Officer Davis working crowd control. She ducked under the yellow tape marking the parade route, stepped over the snow bank, and ran out into the street.

"I'm sorry, Joy, but you'll have to stay behind the tape. The parade will be starting any minute," Officer Davis told her. The clock in the town hall tower struck two, and Joy could hear the drums of the high school band starting their beat.

"I know, Dan," Joy insisted, "but you need to come with me. I figured it out. I know what happened last weekend, and what is probably happening right now. We have to get over to 509 West Elm Street. Now!" She turned and looked up the street. The parade was just coming around the corner of the town hall. Wendell had his tripod set up, ready to take pictures.

"Wendell," she called. "Bring your camera and come with us!"

Wendell turned and looked at her as if she were crazy.

"Believe me, Wendell. This is one exclusive you will not want to miss."

Officer Davis led her to his police car, and with Wendell in the back seat, they sped down Elm Street. Along the way, Joy explained their errand.

"I would never have figured it out without your headline on Thursday, Wendell. The answer is in the two Elm streets."

"What was the question?" Officer Davis asked.

"The question is why Watts picked our house to burglarize, and the answer is he thought it was the Kerrigan's. They live at 509 West Elm, and we live at 509 East Elm. He was an out-of-towner, so he didn't realize there was more than one 509 Elm Street."

"Why would he want to go to the Kerrigan's?" Wendell asked as they pulled up to the address.

"Let's ask him," Joy said, pointing to a Santa standing on the Kerrigan's roof trying to open the skylight. Davis got out of the car, and, using the door as a shield, drew his gun. "Police. Put your hands in the air and freeze," he shouted, pointing his gun at Santa. Wendell started snapping pictures out the window. "Joy, I can't get out of here. Open the door for me. I'm missing the shot."

"Stay inside," Davis barked.

Joy opened her door and released Wendell from the back seat.

"Don't shoot," Santa yelled. "I'm unarmed. I don't mean anyone any harm."

"Dr. Barnes?" Wendell said, snapping more pictures. "Is that you?"

Davis called for back-up, and approached the house. "How did you get up there?"

"I have a ladder in the back," Barnes said.

"Okay, then let's walk toward the back, and you come down the ladder, nice and slow."

Officer Davis read him his rights. By the time the back-up arrived, followed by some of the parade crowd, Barnes was in handcuffs, sitting in the back seat of the cruiser. He was spilling his guts, while Wendell took down every word.

"When I got to Kerrigan's house the night of the accident, the old man thought he was a goner. He told me that while he ran his garage, he saved every old coin that came through his till.

He said he had a collection worth over a hundred-thousand dollars under a loose floorboard upstairs, and no one knew about it—not even his sister. He wanted me to make sure his sister got them. From the look of him, I thought he probably wouldn't make it, so I called my old buddy, Harry Watts. We'd, uh, done some work together in the past."

Joy gave Wendell a smug look.

"Anyway, Watts was a screw-up. He went to the wrong house, and he died for his trouble. There isn't even a skylight at that other house."

Joy nodded. "Never has been."

"So you came back today to get the coins?" Wendell asked.

"I tried to get them out of my mind. But I figured that after the coma, Kerrigan wouldn't remember telling me about them. Heck, he might not remember that he had them. So, I figured it was worth a try."

"And you picked today, because everyone would be at the parade," Joy said.

"Yeah. I hate parades, but it seemed like such a big deal in this town that I figured none of the neighbors would be home to see me here. And I dressed as Santa because Watts said if he did that and moved around like a robot, anyone who saw him would think he was just a mechanical Christmas decoration. It sounded like a good idea to me."

Joy rolled her eyes. "We may be small town, but we're not idiots."

"You didn't have to go to all that trouble," Davis said. "Like too many people in this town, the Kerrigans never lock their doors. You could have just gone inside."

***

The following Thursday, the *Town Monitor* sold every copy. "Caught Red-Suited," read another of Wendell's classic headlines. But the story of Dr. Barnes' criminal ways did not end in their small town. The Springfield police came up to talk to him while he sat in county jail. It looked like Dr. Barnes would not be celebrating Christmas without bars on his windows for a very long time.

"Now, what was that you were saying about me having an over-active imagination?" Joy said, handing the paper to Nick.

"I guess it turned out to be a good thing that you do," Nick said with a wink.

"Uh, you guys," Holly said. "You know you still owe me an ice cream soda."

A Visit from Belsnickel

"*Fröhliche Weihnachten*, Jacob!" The blacksmith clapped a mighty hand on the nine-year-old boy's back, nearly knocking him over. "Happy Christmas to you and your family."

"And the same to you, *Herr* Huber." Jacob pulled off the warm woolen hat his mother had made and stood as tall as he could. "I've brought you some wood from Papa's wagon." Jacob was small for his age but tried to sound grown up. "He is over on Walnut Street delivering wood at the end of the road." Laughing, he added, "Mr. Allen wanted wood, but Papa said his wood was too good for a Tory."

"Mr. Allen is English, so we shouldn't be surprised that he hopes the British will win this war," Mr. Huber said, stroking his bearded chin. "We whose families come from elsewhere aren't so loyal to the British King George." Mr. Huber grabbed logs from Jacob's sled as if they were nothing more than kindling. "Here, let me help you."

"With my Uncle Martin and Uncle Peter in General Washington's army, the Patriots are sure to win," Jacob said, lugging wood inside the *Schmiede*—the German word for a blacksmith shop.

"God bless them and protect them," Mr. Huber said, stacking the wood Jacob brought him. "And I am sure you are a big help to your father, now that your uncles have left the farm."

Jacob wasn't sure how to answer, so he just nodded and turned his sled to go for more wood from Papa's wagon.

When Mr. Huber's shed was full, Jacob said good-bye.

"Oh, Jacob," the blacksmith said, looking at him sideways. "I hope you've been a good boy this year. Belsnickel must be coming soon, *ja?*"

Jacob cringed. He knew Belsnickel, one of St. Nicholas's helpers, came to visit children a few days before Christmas each year. But unlike kindly St. Nicholas, whose feast day they celebrated early in December, Belsnickel was a little scary. He had a black beard and a dark fur cloak and horns on his head. In one hand he carried a sack of nuts and sweets for good children, but in the other he held a wooden switch.

Mr. Huber arched an eyebrow when he saw Jacob's expression. "You *have* been good this year, haven't you, Jacob?"

"Well, uh . . ." Jacob started. He knew he would have to be honest when Belsnickel asked the same question, and there had been many times this year when he hadn't measured up. Like the time Mama sent him to weed the kitchen garden, and he pulled up all the onions by mistake. Or when he forgot to feed the horses, and they went hungry until Papa reminded him. Then there was the time he walked along the fence rail and tore a hole in his breeches when he fell off. He knew he argued with his four-year-old brother Christian more times than Mama could count. Worst of all was the time he lied to Papa, saying he had brought water to the corn when he hadn't. Afterward, some of the corn stalks dried up and died. All while Papa was counting on him to do the work that his uncles used to do. He tried, but . . .

Jacob looked at the floor. "Well, I have tried to be good," he said.

"I hope so," the big man growled. "Or else, you know what will happen."

Jacob rubbed his backside, thinking about Belsnickel's switch. Looking up, he saw Mr. Huber wipe a smile away with his large, calloused hand. Jacob didn't think a whipping was anything to smile about.

Jacob pulled his sled back to Papa's wagon in the half-light of dusk. Daylight ended so early near Christmas that some of their work had to be done after dark.

Papa clicked to the horses, *Braun* and *Schwartz*—so named because one was brown and one was black. The bells on the horses' harness jingled as they trotted through the snow, making Jacob ache for a Christmas like all the ones before.

He knew this year was different. They were at war with England which made goods from overseas hard to get. His uncles would not be home, and the cold had driven the wolves toward the farms as the needs of their stomachs outweighed their fear of humans. The packs had already shrunk the herds of deer, and Jacob knew there would be no venison for dinner this Christmas. Keeping the livestock safe from the marauding wolf pack was all a farmer could hope to do this season.

Papa turned to Jacob. "You did a good job today, Jacob," he said. "Many people will stay warm at Christmas because of the wood we delivered today. Does that not give you a warm feeling inside, too?"

"Yes, Papa," Jacob said, looking at his lap.

"So, what is bothering you, *Sohn?*"

"Nothing, Papa," Jacob said picking up his head and looking out past the horses' hindquarters. Jacob knew he shouldn't complain when his house was warm and his family had enough to eat. Many people, including soldiers like his uncles, had less this winter.

As they neared the farm, Jacob saw the first of the big, fluffy snowflakes. He stuck out his tongue, trying to capture one as it fell, but they swirled on the breeze and were hard to catch.

"Don't fall off the wagon, *Sohn,*" Papa said. "I think there will be plenty of snowflakes to catch when we get home."

"Will it be a big storm, Papa?"

Papa looked at the dark sky. "It's hard to be sure ahead of time. We'll see how long it lasts. But we made our deliveries, so we won't need to take the wagon out tomorrow."

Jacob had a thought. "Papa, we only have three days until Christmas, right?"

"Let's see now." Jacob could tell Papa was only pretending not to know. "I believe it is three days away." Papa kept one hand on the reins but ruffled Jacob's cap with the other.

"So, Belsnickel must be coming *very* soon."

Papa shook his head. "He comes without warning," he said, clearing his throat. "But this year, it might be hard for him to get through."

Jacob didn't know whether to be disappointed or relieved. "Why, Papa?"

Papa coughed and looked straight ahead. "He travels overland, you know, Jacob."

Jacob nodded. "But he came last year, didn't he?"

Papa shrugged one shoulder. "True. But this year there is a war, and he might be stopped by British soldiers if he tries to come to Pennsylvania. The English are camped nearby in New Jersey, and they do not like Belsnickel."

Could he really be stopped by English soldiers? Jacob wondered. He had always thought of Belsnickel as being sort of magical.

As the horses drew the wagon toward their barn, Papa pulled on the reins and the wagon stopped. "Now open the barn door, then go into the house and ask Mama for two lanterns. I will lead the wagon inside," Papa said.

Jacob jumped down and slid the heavy wooden door until it was open wide enough for the horses and wagon to pass through. Then he tromped to the house, wishing he knew what to make of Belsnickel's predicament.

Mama let Jacob take a long sliver of kindling to light the tallow candles inside two punched-tin lanterns. The lanterns didn't yield much light, but they were the safest kind to have in a barn. The holes in the tin were small, but they let enough air in to keep the candle lit without allowing a gust of wind to blow the candle out. And unlike a glass lantern that could break and start a fire in the hay, the metal lantern kept the fire safely inside. The light showing through the holes made pretty designs on the walls—just for nice. If the candle inside were too long, though, the lantern would get too hot to carry by its round, metal handle on top, so they always used short candle nubs.

Papa had finished unhitching Schwartz and Braun and had them on cross-ties by the time Jacob returned. Jacob grabbed a brush and started working on their legs and bellies while Papa brushed their backs and sides. As Papa worked above him, Jacob picked the snow and dirt out of their wide hooves.

All the while, he worried about Belsnickel. He didn't want a switching, but it wouldn't seem like Christmas without his visit. Poor Christian wouldn't have a chance to get the nuts and candy he brought. And if someone as strong and mean as Belsnickel couldn't get past the British soldiers, what chance would *Christkind* have to bring them gifts on Christmas Eve? Jacob sighed. The Christ child might bring Christian a toy, but Jacob thought he would only get a rock.

Still, Christmas was a special time for family to be together. He missed his uncles who always played games with him and made Christmas fun. Uncle Peter was particularly good at molding figures of Mary, Joseph, baby Jesus, shepherds, and wise men out of clay for the *Putz*. Jacob felt a lump in his throat, and his eyes burned with tears. He wiped his sleeve across his face.

"Are you all right?" Papa asked. Jacob heard concern in his voice and sniffed back his tears.

"My eyes burn from the tallow candle," Jacob said.

"Then move the lantern farther away," Papa said as he kept brushing Braun.

Jacob did so, but while working in the dark, he began to develop a plan.

When the horses were cooled down, fed, and watered, Papa brushed his hands together. "Shall we go in and find out what good supper Mama has waiting for us?"

Jacob hesitated. "Would it be okay if I stay here a little while? I have something I want to do."

Papa squinted at him. "That sounds very mysterious, young man."

Jacob looked up with what he hoped was a winning smile.

Papa grinned. "Just don't get into any mischief. You know Bel . . . well, you should be especially good this time of year."

"I will be, Papa," Jacob said in his most responsible voice.

"Don't be too long. Supper should be on the table soon." Papa left, taking one of the lanterns with him.

There wasn't much time, but Jacob knew he could at least get started on his idea. He looked around for something he could use as a fur coat. There was an old cowhide that Papa had dried. It was stiff and way too big for Jacob. That wouldn't work. Then he found a bin filled with some dirty sheep's wool from the last shearing. Maybe he could stick some on his coat and make it look like a fur.

But the fleece was not black like Belsnickel's fur coat. He could probably find a way to make it black. No—he'd better not. He knew Mama would clean and card the wool this winter, and they would spin it into yarn to weave into cloth for their clothes. She would want white fleece so she could dye it to whatever color she wanted. And how would he stick it on without ruining both it and his coat?

Next, he found deer antlers and decided he could tie them to his head with his hat down over his eyes so no one could see who he was. And a sack for nuts and candy would be no problem. Papa had lots of old sacks. Cutting a switch should be easy, too. Finding nuts would be hard in the snow, though. And making candies would be nearly impossible.

But hardest of all was convincing Christian that a smallish boy was the fearsome Belsnickel. Maybe he wouldn't remember the big man who came last year and be so surprised to see Belsnickel pounding at his door that he wouldn't wonder about how big he was. He wanted at least to try.

His candle sputtered and went out, and the smell of animal fat emanated from the lantern. Jacob had to find his way into the house in the dark. There was nothing more he could do tonight.

* * *

Jacob woke early the next morning and dressed quickly to get out to the barn before Papa came in to take care of the animals. When he looked outside, he saw that it was still snowing and that the path to the barn already had over a foot of snow. He couldn't even see any dents in the snow where he had walked the night before.

He grabbed the shovel by the door and started to clear the path. Before he had gone more than a few feet, Papa came up behind him.

"Good job, *Sohn*," he said. "Now it's my turn." Papa grabbed the shovel and plowed through the snow in long, wide arcs, moving more snow in two or three shovelfuls than Jacob had moved all morning.

When they got to the barn door and cleaned out the snow that had drifted there, they were able to slide the door open just enough to duck inside.

The barn was dark compared to the white world outside, but it was warmer, too, and smelled of hay and corn and molasses and animals. It was a smell Jacob loved.

Schwartz nickered as they came into the barn. Jacob bounded over to his stall and patted his velvety nose. The horse raised his head, and Jacob could no longer reach his muzzle. "Okay," Jacob said. "I know how to get you to lower your head. Put something in your feed bucket."

After they had finished tending to the animals, Papa patted his belly. "I'm ready for your Mama's good breakfast," he said with a gleam in his eye. "Come on, boy."

Jacob looked around and spied some wool fleece that he had left out of place. He knew he was running out of time. Tonight was the last night Belsnickel could come because tomorrow night was Christmas Eve. But Mama's good cooking called to his empty stomach, so he followed Papa out the door.

More snow had fallen while they were in the barn. Jacob tried to step into Papa's footprints in the new snow. Papa's legs were long, but Jacob's were short, and he fell when trying to keep up. It took him twice as long as Papa to get from the barn to the house, and when he arrived, Papa turned to him and laughed.

"You look like a man made of snow," he said, taking off Jacob's hat and shaking it clean. "Now brush off your coat and stomp your boots. Mama won't want puddles in the house."

Jacob did as he was told, and followed Papa into the house. The smell of *wurst* and apple pancakes made his stomach complain. He couldn't get his coat and boots off fast enough to quiet it. After the blessing, he waited for Papa to take the first bite, then ate so quickly, he forgot to savor the flavors and spices. But his stomach was glad he hadn't waited any longer.

"Do you need my help, Papa?" Jacob asked when their plates were empty.

Papa looked from him to Christian and back. "Not until it's time to feed the animals again," he said. "You can stay and play with your brother if you would like."

Jacob looked at Christian, hoping he hadn't heard. But he had. Christian jumped from his chair and pulled at Jacob's elbow.

"We can play in the snow," Christian squealed.

Jacob got up and pulled on his boots, and Christian began to do the same.

"I'll try to play with you later, Christian," he said. The little boy's expression changed from glee to disappointment. His lower lip jutted out and began to quiver.

"Why, Jacob? Papa said you could play with me now."

"But I still have some work to do before I can play," he explained.

"Do you have to feed the animals?" Christian asked with a whine in his voice.

"Not yet, but I still have to . . ."

"Do you have to move more firewood?"

"Not today, but there are still things . . ."

"Then *why* can't you play with me?" Christian was close to tears.

Jacob took a deep breath. "There is some work I need to do that cannot wait," he explained with all the patience he could muster. "But I will come back as soon as I can, and we'll see if there is time to play then." He didn't yell at Christian as he might have any other day. He felt very grown up.

"After dinner," Mama said, "we're going to make gingerbread men. I will need your help then, Jacob."

"Oh, good. We can play after dinner," Christian was happy again.

"Yes, Mama," Jacob said, knowing that helping with the baking is a child's job. He was doing a man's work now, but he couldn't disobey. And it would give him a chance to keep his promise to his brother.

Returning to the barn, he looked around until he found a sack that was just the right size for the few treats he could carry. Then he dug through the wool to see how much he had to work with. The sheep were shorn so that their fleece was one big piece. The wool held together, bound by snarls and sticks and leaves and dirt.

Working with it, Jacob found his hands getting a little sticky, but his rough knuckles and red skin felt smoother than before. He remembered Mama said that was why she liked to work with wool in the winter. It made her skin soft.

He looked for some sort of glue he could use that wouldn't ruin his coat or the wool. There was tar that Papa used on the horses' hooves, but that was too black and impossible to clean. Besides, in the cold, it was too hard to use. He would have to warm it by the fireside, and that would raise questions. Looking around, he found turpentine—no that would not work, either. Maybe some clay? No, too dirty and not sticky enough.

"Isn't there anything I can use?" he asked Braun, who stood watching him from his stall. He tried one thing after another. Finally, he tried draping some of the wool over his shoulders. He decided that if it held together, he could tuck it around his collar, in his hat, and in his pockets and sleeves. That ought to look enough like a fur coat to fool Christian if he could stay in the dark. Maybe he could make Christian blow out the candles when he came in the door.

It was time for the mid-day dinner, and he still needed to cut a switch and find some nuts. He should have those even if he couldn't make any candies. Then he'd use Papa's string to tie on the antlers. He would have to wait and work on those after helping with the baking.

As he left the barn, he noticed that the snow had stopped, but the clouds overhead were thick and gray. The walk from the barn to the house felt longer every time he went out. The snow was deep, and his feet were wet and cold. He couldn't wait to take off his boots and warm his feet by the fire.

Jacob smelled the dinner stew as soon as he opened the door. They sat at the table together and warmed their insides with root vegetables, mutton, and gravy. Mama's biscuits were light and flaky. Papa said she was the best cook in the whole country. Jacob was sure he was right.

After the dishes had been cleared away, Papa went outside, and they went to work on the gingerbread. Mama had already made the cookie dough. Now she rolled it and cut it into cookies shaped like little men. Christian and Jacob sat at the trestle table and placed raisins on the cookies to be their eyes and the buttons down their bellies. Then Mama pushed aside the embers in the brick oven, and slid the cookies inside to bake. Jacob loved the smell of gingerbread. It smelled like Christmas. For a few minutes, he forgot about his project in the barn.

Soon they had a stack of tasty cookies. One of the gingerbread men broke when it came out of the oven, and Mama let the boys share it. As Jacob tasted his first bite, there was a big thump on the porch and a loud knocking at the door. Could it be Belsnickel coming during the day? Jacob ran to the door and opened it to a mass of green fir branches.

"Grab the end, Jacob, and let us get this monster into the house," Papa said from behind the tree. Jacob bent over and pulled on the branches to help Papa get the tree through the door.

Christian clapped his hands and laughed when Papa closed the door and held the tree upright.

"Papa!" Mama said. "You are dropping snow on the floor and making puddles in the house."

Papa raised an eyebrow to Jacob as if to say, "I told you she wouldn't like that."

Jacob laughed and wiped snow off the floor while Papa placed the tree in front of the window. It stood nearly as tall as Papa, and because it blocked the window, it made it darker in the house. The room took on the yellow-orange glow of the kitchen fire.

After the cookies cooled, they all hung gingerbread men on the tree. Mama had a many-pointed star of tin that Papa placed at the very top of the tree. It was beautiful.

Papa sang out *"O Tannenbaum,"* and Jacob and Mama joined in. Christian tried to sing, too, but he was too young and didn't know all the words.

Then, with a start, Jacob realized he still had more work to do in the barn and needed to go out to the woods to find some nuts and cut a switch. He pulled on his coat and boots and told his parents he would be back soon.

He stepped outside and realized that it was already nearly dark and snow had started to fall again. He went into the barn and stuffed wool in and around his coat. He attached string to the antlers and tried to tie them to his head. They were wobbly, and wouldn't stay on very long, so he took them off and decided to put them on just before he knocked on the door. He trudged out through the snow into the nearby woods to dig for black walnuts and to find the perfect switch.

By the time he reached the walnut trees, the snow was deep. No moon shone through the dense storm clouds, and Jacob could hardly see the trees around him. He fell to his knees and pawed into the snow, digging as hard as he could. His hands were freezing inside his gloves, and his toes were even colder. Still, he dug and dug until he found several frozen husks—but they were empty. Squirrels had already harvested most of the black walnuts.

After digging more, he found a few brown and light green husks, frozen solid, with their precious walnuts safe inside. He planned to use Papa's hammer and smash the husks in the barn to get the walnuts out without dirtying his hands with their black walnut stain. He gathered as many as he could in the dark and snow, and put them in one of Papa's sacks.

As he stood up, he heard something moving in the trees. He stopped and held his breath. He felt like he was being watched. Could it be some wolves that were looking for an early Christmas dinner? He panicked when he realized that the wool he was wearing made him smell like a sheep.

He tried to calm himself as he backed away from the sound. He knew wolves hunted in packs. He could never outrun one wolf, let alone a pack of them. And running would only make them want to chase him and bring him down. Jacob had no doubt they could do just that.

He tried to make out the shape of the house on the other side of the clearing, silhouetted against the snow. Small sparks of light hit the snowy ground, shining from the window that was mostly blocked by Papa's big tree. He would have to get through the woods and across the clearing to be safe.

Or maybe he should climb a tree. Jacob knew wolves couldn't climb trees. He also knew that wolves could stay under a tree until their prey either came back down for food or fell out when they went to sleep. And if he stayed outside too long, the cold would get him even if the wolves did not.

He had no choice. He would have to back slowly toward the house and hope the wolves wouldn't chase him if he didn't run.

He tried to retrace his steps, looking backwards from the corner of his eye to find his footprints. It was too dark to see more than one step at a time. His heart pounded, but he had to proceed slowly. If he fell, the wolves could be on him before he could stand up again.

As he approached the clearing, he could smell the wood smoke from the chimney. He felt like running toward the flecks of light that showed him where the house was. But he still needed a switch.

He found some frozen saplings lining the field and tried to cut one of the larger ones. It would be a very respectable switch for Belsnickel, and might even help fend off a wolf if need be. But the sapling was too thick and too frozen for his knife to penetrate the wood. He tried a smaller one, but it was also shorter—too short for Belsnickel's switch. Still, it was better than nothing.

He sawed with his knife, but he wasn't making much progress. He tried just breaking the stick, hoping the cold had made the green wood brittle. It hadn't.

He didn't want to stay where he was much longer. He still felt watched. Then he heard a growl.

He thought of yelling for help, but he was too far from the house to be heard. He tried anyway.

"Heeeeelp!" he yelled. Maybe yelling would scare the wolves he was now sure were following him. In the dark, he thought he saw movement to his side. Were they surrounding him?

C-r-a-a-a-a-c-k! A loud noise like a whip exploded next to him, followed by a rustling in the trees. A big hand grabbed him under his arm and pulled him up. The next thing he knew, he was being carried over someone's shoulder, and they were making quick work of crossing the field toward the barn.

The big man holding him opened the barn door and plopped Jacob inside. When Jacob looked up, the man appeared almost as big as the barn door itself.

"What were you doing out there?" a booming voice echoed in the quiet stable. The startled horses whinnied and stirred in their stalls.

Jacob couldn't see the face of the giant who asked the question, but there was no doubt in his mind who it was.

"I was afraid the British soldiers would keep you from coming this year, sir," Jacob said in short bursts of breath. "I tried to make sure my brother Christian could still get his treats. But I have no fur coat and no horns, no switch, no candy, and the walnuts I found are all frozen." He hung his head. "I guess I wasn't a very good imitation of you."

"You? Imitate me?" Belsnickel growled the words. "Is this wool supposed to be my fur coat?"

"Yes, sir," Jacob said, not daring to look at him.

"And those deer antlers, are they supposed to be my horns?"

"They were the only things I could find." Jacob pulled up his shoulders to protect his head from a beating. But in a moment, Jacob thought he heard Belsnickel's growl become a laugh deep in his belly.

"Get rid of this wool, and empty your sack of those frozen walnuts. Then go in the house.

Do not tell anyone that I am here. I will knock shortly."

Jacob returned the wool to the bin, cleared away the antlers, and removed the walnuts from the sack.

Belsnickel stood aside and let Jacob out of the barn. He ran to the house with a mixture of fear and relief. As soon as he entered, both his parents and Christian stared at him. He couldn't tell them what had happened, so he just stood there leaning against the door, when a loud banging nearly knocked him to the floor.

"Who could that be?" asked Mama.

"I don't know. It's late for visitors," said Papa.

"It's Belsnickel," Jacob said and ran from the door to stand behind Mama.

Papa opened the door. His eyes grew large, and his mouth hung open.

"Let me see the children," Belsnickel ordered Papa.

"Of . . . of course," Papa said. "Boys, come here and meet our visitor."

Jacob stayed behind Mama, and Christian hid behind Jacob.

"*Kinder*, come here," Belsnickel said. "If you have been good, there is nothing to fear. Have you been good this year?"

Christian nodded his head but didn't make a sound. Jacob knew it made no sense to lie to Belsnickel.

"No," he said, stepping out to face Belsnickel. "I have tried, but I have not always been as good as I should have been," Jacob confessed.

Belsnickel turned his head and looked at Jacob out of the corner of his eye. Something about his expression looked familiar. Then Belsnickel raised his switch and cracked it against the floor in front of him. Jacob winced and stepped back.

"Young Jacob," Belsnickel said, in a voice that sounded almost kind. "I tried to give you a switching, but my aim wasn't as good as it should have been. Does that make me a bad Belsnickel?"

Jacob shook his head. "No, you're . . ." Jacob thought a moment, and realized what Belsnickel might be saying. "Do you mean that no one is perfect all the time, no matter how hard they try?"

"No one can be," Belsnickel said. "Not even adults. Everyone makes mistakes. As long as they admit it, apologize, and try to do better, they are still good people."

Jacob turned that around in his head. "Good" didn't have to mean "perfect."

"You have made your mistakes," Belsnickel continued, "but you have helped your father while your uncles are at war. You have tried to do the work of men. And you have tried to make a good Christmas for your brother."

Jacob nodded. All that was true.

"So I am asking you again, have you been good this year?"

Jacob still thought about the times he should have been better, but he turned to Belsnickel and said, "I have not been perfect, Herr Belsnickel, but I have been good."

"Good. Can you recite for me the twenty-third Psalm?"

Jacob recited the Bible passage. When he got to the part about, "though I walk through the Valley of the Shadow of Death, I shall fear no evil, for Thou art with me," he thought about the wolves. He looked up at Belsnickel and knew that despite his scary appearance and gruff manner, underneath it all, he was good-hearted.

Belsnickel put some candy and cakes and nuts on the floor. Christian leaped upon them, but Papa pulled him back. "Ask permission first, *Sohn,*" Papa said.

"*Bitte,* may I have some?" Christian asked. Belsnickel nodded, and Mama let Christian pick up two pieces of candy, one cake, and three nuts. It was all his little hands could hold.

Belsnickel eyed Jacob. "Don't you want some?" he asked.

Jacob thought about how, if it weren't for Belsnickel, he might have been dinner for a wolf pack instead of home with his family in his snug house with its beautiful Christmas tree.

"Well . . .," Jacob said. He looked around the room. Christian lined up his treats on the table. Mama gave Belsnickel a cup of hot cider to warm him before he went back out in the snow, and Papa hung Jacob's coat and gloves by the fire to dry. He felt a warm Christmas love build in his heart.

"No thank you, sir. You have given me enough," Jacob said. "Give these to other children. My riches are great enough without them."

"Will you stay and help us light candles on the Christmas tree?" Christian asked Belsnickel.

The big man shook his head. "No. I have other homes to visit. But you be good, *Junge,* because I'll be back next year." He handed Mama his empty cup and picked up his pack and his switch.

"Thank you, Herr Belsnickel," Jacob said as the giant opened their door. "Thank you . . . for everything."

Belsnickel winked at Jacob and trudged out into the snow.

Jacob waved as he left. "Good-bye until next year," he called.

He heard a big belly laugh coming from the darkness and could barely see Belsnickel raise his hand to wave back at him. But he could clearly hear him call, "*Fröhliche Weihnachten,* Jacob!"

And it was—a very happy Christmas, indeed.

###

Author's Note

I love writing short stories because they allow a writer to experiment in different genres and styles. Writing various themes, voices, or length requirements provides opportunies to stretch my craft. What I didn't realize until putting this collection together, is that no matter what genre, no matter what length, no matter what theme, my stories all contain family connections. Some characters are snarky, some sentimental, but each is part of a family that they want to preserve or protect.

I have been honored to have versions of each of these stories previously published in a variety of venues, as follows:

"A Christmas on Nantucket," "Dora's Chocolate Cake" (under the title "Nana's Chocolate Cake), and "You Better Watch Out," in *A Christmas Sampler: Sweet, Funny, and Strange Holiday Tales,* Bethlehem Writers Group (2009). Winner of "Best Short Fiction" and "Best Anthology" in the 2010 Next Generation Indie

Book Awards. "A Christmas on Nantucket" also appeared in *Write Here, Write Now,* Greater Lehigh Valley Writers Group (2016).

"We Gather Together" and "Summer Nights," in Bethlehem Writers Roundtable, Issue 14, November, 2012.

"My First Red Sox Game," in *Once Around the Sun: Sweet, Funny, and Strange Tales for All Seasons,* Bethlehem Writers Group, LLC (2014). Finalist, 2015 Next Generation Indie Book Awards.

"American Flyers," in *Let It Snow: The Best of Bethlehem Writers Roundtable, Winter 2015 Collection,* Bethlehem Writers Group, LLC (2015). This story originally appeared in "Bethlehem Writers Roundtable," Bethlehem Writers Group, LLC, Issue 28, January, 2014.

"The Hunt" and "Grandma's Vegetable Soup" (under the title "Nana's Vegetable Soup") in *A Readable Feast: Sweet, Funny, and Strange Tales for Every Taste,* Bethlehem Writers Group, LLC (2014). Finalist, 2015 Next Generation Indie Book Awards.

"Maddie's Birthday Surprise" and "A Visit from Belsnickel," in *Once Upon a Time: Sweet, Funny, and Strange Tales for All Ages* (2015).

"Connecting the Dots," in *The Write Connections: 2017 GLVWG Anthology,* Greater Lehigh Valley Writers Group (2017).

"Dark Side of the Light" in *Day of the Dark: Stories of Eclipse,* Kaye George, ed., Wildside Books (2017).

"A Late Afternoon Visitor," "A Mother's Gift," "The Dream," and "The Man from Hooverville" in *Untethered: Sweet, Funny, and Strange Tales of the Paranormal* (2018). Finalist, 2019 Killer Nashville Silver Falchion Award. "The Man from Hooverville" has been adapted as a musical, "Always With Us," book and music by Paula G. Benson (2019).

I extend heartfelt thanks to all those who have helped me with the creative process over the years, most especially the members of the Bethlehem Writers Group who are always generous with their advice and support.

In addition, I know I can never sufficiently thank my weird and wonderful family for their unflagging inspiration and support. As you can tell from my stories, family is important to me—the whole bunch (including in-laws)—grandparents, parents, siblings, spouse, children, and grandchildren. I am eternally grateful for being blessed with a creative, caring, challenging, curious, and never-boring clan of characters.

About the Author

Carol L. Wright escaped a career in law and academia for one in writing. She loves writing her Gracie McIntyre cozy mysteries where, unlike in life, justice always prevails. The first in the series, *Death in Glenville Falls,* was a finalist for both the 2018 Killer Nashville Silver Falchion Award and a 2018 Next Generation Indie Book Award. She also writes short stories in many genres that have been published in a variety of literary journals and award-winning anthologies. She is married to her college sweetheart. They are the parents to two adult children and grandparents of two. They live in the Lehigh Valley of Pennsylvania with their rescue dog and clowder of cats. Find out more on her website, http://CarolLWright.com, and on Facebook at Carol L. Wright, Author.

Also from

Carol L. Wright

Death in Glenville Falls

A Gracie McIntyre Mystery

Finalist for
2018 Killer Nashville Silver Falchion Award
Best Cozy Mystery

Finalist for a
2018 Next Generation Indie Book Award

Paperback ISBN: 978-0-9742891-3-7
Ebook ISBN: 978-0-9742891-4-4